All Girls Should Know How to Braid

All Girls Should Know How to Braid

Tonya Holloway

iUniverse, Inc.
New York Bloomington

All Girls Should Know How to Braid

iUniverse books may be ordered through booksellers or by contacting:

iUniverse
1663 Liberty Drive
Bloomington, IN 47403
www.iuniverse.com
1-800-Authors (1-800-288-4677)

ISBN: 978-1-4502-1121-5 (sc)
ISBN: 978-1-4502-1122-2 (ebk)

Printed in the United States of America

iUniverse rev. date: 3/29/2010

For my Parents who gave me Imagination

To my sisters who Inspire

To S.V who is unconditional Love

Chapter One

The year was 1983 and everybody was "Beating It" with Michael Jackson, who at the time was the biggest pop star on the planet. Almost every girl had their legs covered with legwarmers; long open-toed socks usually worn by dancers. Florescent sweatshirts were popular like the one seen in the movie *Flashdance,* and Penny Loafers, brown leather shoes with a penny tucked in the middle, were making a comeback. They had been out of style for a couple of years, but when some actors from a popular T.V. show were seen wearing them each week, the fad was re-born. If you were really cool and could afford it, quarters were placed in the middle of the slot on top of the shoe instead of pennies. One time I saved up two quarters to put in my Penny Loafers but ended up taking them out to buy some ice cream from the corner store. That was the end of my Quarter Loafer days. Pennies would have to do. But the style of all styles was a Jheri Curl, and everyone, girls and boys, had a Jheri Curl. Everyone except me, Stacy Bell.

You see, if you had a Jheri Curl, you had to put glycerin in your hair to make it curl; a lot of glycerin. My Mama didn't like the greasiness of the style. She said glycerin was too messy and thought people paid too much money just to put a curl in their hair. *Rule #63: Only simple, natural hairstyles will be worn by children while they are in my house.* "Ponytails look better," she'd say. Whatever was "in" for the new school year usually meant I wore what was "out" from last year. That's pretty much how I accepted things until seventh grade. Fate was calling roll and for the first time, my name was at the top of the list.

The September fall morning began like any other day. On my street, everyone had routines. Mothers prepared their kids for school and Dads or teenage boys, took out the trash; except for Mr. J. Being a single parent, he did both. He could even do his daughters' hair! I couldn't help but stare the first time I saw him part, grease, plait and accessorized their hair with colored ribbons and berets before giving us a ride to school. Boy, was that unusual.

The middle-class homes were different in sizes, shapes and colors. The lawns were always sculpted like perfectly painted pictures of green lawns in the summer, a mixture of brown, orange and red trees in the fall and frosted grass glistening from the sun rays in the winter. We didn't have the best stores or places to eat in my neighborhood, but what we had was familiar and enough.

Forest Hill Middle School was nothing special to look at from the outside. It was old like the houses around it, unlike the ones a few streets over. There were no pretty flowers planted in specific spots on the front lawn, nor a fancy sign displaying our school name and mascot. The classrooms and auditorium smelled of old wood and musty outdated books. The cafeteria was small and plain and no matter what was on the menu, it always carried the scent of chicken fried steak with mashed potatoes.

Even though it wasn't the top middle school in the city, most kids from my block wanted to attend because of its rep. We had the best basketball, football and track teams. The little kids would envy the older ones in the neighborhood who talked about the latest events that went-down on the "Hill" and couldn't wait for the day they too would brag about their own stories.

The night before my first day of school at Forest Hill Middle, I was so excited and nervous I couldn't sleep. Since fifth grade, I had been waiting for the day I would step foot into the schoolyard not as a visitor but as a student. But like a toy you get for Christmas, after awhile, the newness wore off. Once I got a schedule, learned my way around and found out which teachers were hard and which ones were easy, the excitement went away.

Some mornings, I arrived at school early because Granny was driving instead of Mama. Granny was early for everything. She always told stories about how she and her sisters and brothers had to get up early to start their daily chores before school. "We got up so early, we had to walk to daylight," she'd say.

I didn't mind being early. It gave me a chance to eat a second breakfast in the school cafeteria. Unlike the one I ate at home, this breakfast was a choice of jelly-filled donuts, chocolate milk and my favorite: fried cherry pies. It also gave me a chance to watch the cutest eighth grade boy get off of bus 271.

His name was Herman Price. I noticed him from the first day of school. He had a coolness that made him stand out from the other class clowns he hung around, *and* he was smart. He was the only boy in school with hazel-green eyes. I studied him well, but to him, I was invisible. You had to be pretty or athletic or tough for an eighth grader to notice a seventh grader , and I wasn't any of those things.

Still, I used to love to see him glide off the bus and walk over with his buddies to what was known as "The Wall." I looked forward to seeing what he would wear and how he styled his hair. Would his extra curly Jheri Curl have a part on the side or be picked out in a small curly afro?

Once he got to The Wall, he and his friends would drop their book bags and assume the position. They would lean back with one leg on the ground, and the other propped up against the faded brick wall. Their arms were hugged around their chest like rappers ready to hit the stage. The final touch to their famous pose was a slight tilt of the head to the right. That meant you were super cool. Only the popular eighth grade boys stood by The Wall. With my best friend Tomika, I always made sure to stay a safe distance from their sight.

Tomika and I had been friends since the sixth grade, but I didn't have her popularity. Everybody knew Tomika because she could run fast. She was the only seventh grader on the Varsity track team. Her fame came one summer in the back of her apartments when she raced some popular girls from school and smoked them. After that, she became a known name. And, of course, she had a Jheri Curl.

I always thought Tomika was the better-looking one in our duo. She reminded me of a Black version of Betty Boop. Her body had blossomed much earlier than most girls in our class, which I envied. Her eyes were doe-like with long black eyelashes and the smell of her mom's favorite rose scented potpourri covered every place she stood. Her glossy mouth was permanently shaped in a pucker, as if she was always ready for a kiss and a tube of cherry flavored lip gloss could always be found in a secret compartment of her backpack. When out of her mom's sight, she'd slap on two layers before getting off the bus, flip up her collar and step into the schoolyard as a bona fide undercover Fly Girl.

I waited in my usual spot for the buses to arrive. Tomika's bus pulled up to the curb. She stepped off and immediately noticed me standing in our meeting area. As always, Tomika was wearing a bad outfit. Not bad as in ugly bad, but bad as in I-wish-I-had-one-just-like-it bad. It seemed like she had a new outfit every week. Maybe if I dressed like Tomika I could get Herman's attention.

"Hey girl. I like your jogging suit," I said.

"Thanks. My sister bought it for me yesterday. You can wear it next week if you want."

"Naw," I said. "My Mama don't like me wearing other people's clothes. Besides, everyone would know it's not mine." *Rule #25: We don't borrow other people's clothes.* Tomika looked off toward The Wall and noticed her brother.

"There's my knot-head brother. I need my lunch money from him. Come walk over there with me." I grabbed Tomika's arm. Even though we told each other everything, I kept my secret crush on Herman to myself.

"No! I'm not walking over there," I exclaimed.

"Why not? Kasey's not gonna bite you."

"I don't want to walk by The Wall. I'll wait for you here," I said. Tomika looked at The Wall, then back at me. She looked confused for a minute. Then her eyes grew wider with each thought.

"Oooohhhh! You like someone over there," she yelled.

"I do not. I just don't like walking by The Wall. Everybody always stares at you," I said, trying to make up something.

"Stacy, I know you girl. You like somebody over there and if you don't tell me who, I'm gonna have to find out by asking them myself," Tomika threatened.

"You wouldn't do that."

"You know I would," she said with certainty.

"Alright! But if you say anything to anyone we are not friends anymore." I said with a dare in my eyes.

"Deal! Now tell me. Is it Michael Payne?" she eagerly asked. I shook my head no. "Is it Bryson?" Again, I shook my head no. "Kasey?" she said.

"No!" I quickly responded. Tomika stomped her foot.

"Then who? I know it's not the Twins and Eddie is too goofy for anyone to like him. The only one left is Herman and...Ooooh! You like Herman?" she questioned. As soon as I admitted my crush with a smile, I instantly regretted telling the secret.

"Why are you laughing?" I asked.

"Ah I'm not laughing at you. I'm laughing that it's Herman. I didn't think you would like someone like him. But I guess he's a little cute. I never really paid attention. Does he know?" asked Tomika.

I looked at her as if to say, "What you think?"

"I can introduce you to him after school today," she offered.

"Are you crazy? I can't meet him," I said.

"Herman's cool. He's not like those bone heads he hangs around," Tomika said trying to make it sound easy. I thought for a minute. There was a side of me that wanted him to know my true feelings. Who knows, he could turn out to act like the Herman in my dreams. In the dream, he takes one look at me and thinks I'm the prettiest girl in school. He holds my books as we walk down the hallway and even buys my favorite cherry pies at lunch. We pass love notes to each other during class that say, "I think you're cute" and at the end of each day, the rudest girls envy me. But like always, the images in my dream bubble pop, leaving me stuck in reality.

Maybe he wasn't like the rest of the eighth grade boys. Maybe meeting him would make me popular. I would be known as one of the cool seventh graders because I was with "The Herman." As my confidence started to build, I agreed to the plan..

"Okay I'll do it. But don't say I like him. Just act like I don't know what you're doing," I said. But as I started to plan the meeting, I wondered if this was a good idea. It was kinda like one of those moments Mama always warned me about when she would say, *Rule #8: Think before you speak.*

"I know how to pretend," Tomika said and continued the plan with *her* instructions. "So, after school, stand at the- "

"Not after school!" I said in a panic.

"I thought you wanted me to introduce you to him."

"I did. I mean I do, but not today. I'm not ready. Look at me! My Mama made me wear this corny shirt. I can't meet him looking like this!"

"Girl, you look okay. Whacha so afraid of? It's just big head Herman. I said he was cool but he's not *that* cool. Believe me, I know because he hangs around my brother a lot and my brother is goofy," said Tomika.

"Not cool? Have you seen him play basketball? He's really good. He can dribble the ball double time between his legs and he can balance the ball on his first finger like the Harlem Globe Trotters. I know, cause my Dad took me and my brothers to see them last summer," I said, boasting like I had taught him how to play ball myself. Tomika waved me off.

"I can run circles around him. Look, the bell is about to ring. Do you want to meet him or not?" Tomika asked. I decided to take Mama's advice and think about it one more time before giving my answer. Then with a teaspoon of confidence, I said, "Tomorrow. I promise. I'll have on my best clothes, and I'll get Mama to put a Golden Girl perm on my hair. They're cheap and shouldn't take that long to do," I said.

"Okay girl. But you better not chicken out on me or I'll tell him anyway, ready or not," Tomika said with sneaky grin. My heart dropped in my stomach at the thought of him knowing my secret before I had enough time to transform myself.

"Quit playing Tomika," I said.

"Who's playing? I might even slip him a note in sixth period today," she said. Tomika knew by threatening to tell, it would scare me into keeping my word.

"We can meet tomorrow. I promise," I confirmed.

Just then, the bell rang. Everyone shoved their way through the main doors that were too narrow for the countless number of kids entering. The shuffling of bodies made Herman move closer to us. Tomika sudden shout of Herman's name caused me to turn my head quickly away from his view. He nodded as if to say, "What's up?"

"Tell my brother I said meet me at my locker. I need my lunch money," said Tomika. He nodded again and shuffled through the doors with the other boys. He didn't notice me. No one ever did.

Chapter Two

The school day was getting in my way. I wanted it to be over, so I could concentrate on Herman and tomorrow's introduction. There was only a small amount of time to perform a big miracle. I sat with Tomika at lunch as usual, but didn't say much. In between classes, I walked through the halls like a zombie.

Before long, the sixth period bell was ringing. Normally, this was a class I liked for two reasons: first, English was one of my favorite subjects and second, Herman Price also took Mrs. Carter's sixth period class. Since it was honors English, it was a mix of seventh and eighth graders. I guess you could say the best of the best. I remember on the first day of school, Mrs. Carter asked the class one by one to name their favorite author. Everybody was naming someone easy like Judy Bloom or Shakespeare. Yeah right, like we really read Shakespeare over the summer. When it was Herman's turn, he said, F. Scott Fitzgerald. We all turned and looked at him as if the Mothership from Mars had just transported him into our classroom. He went on to say *The Great Gatsby* was one of his favorite books. Mrs. Carter smiled as if she had finally found her prize-winning student. "Excellent Mr. Price!" she proclaimed. "I like that book too!"

Most days, I would sneak glances at Herman throughout class. The dream bubbles would flash in my head and I'd start floating off to Hermanland. But today, my eyes were glued to the board. Even though I knew Tomika hadn't said a word to him yet, the thought of what was to come made me too nervous to look in his direction.

Tomika on the other hand, now knowing my secret, had fun dangling the threat of spilling the goods to Herman. She constantly made kissy faces behind his back and passed "Stacy loves Herman" notes to me. The only set of love notes I wanted were Herman's. Not Tomika's! I bugged my eyes and pressed my lips so tight you would have thought I had just tossed a couple of Lemon Heads in my mouth. I pantomimed the words "*stop it,*" but it was too late. Mrs. Carter caught us. I swear that woman had a third eye hidden behind her right ear.

She stopped and looked at us with an icy glare. "Miss Stacy Bell, do you have something important to say?" she asked. I could hear small giggles from across the room. I was so embarrassed I could hardly speak.

"Ma'am?" I squeaked.

"You and Miss Sanders seem to be engaged in a conversation that evidently is more important than what I have to tell the class. Please, enlighten us."

Silence covered the room louder than afternoon announcements. Everyone was waiting for my answer. I vowed right then never to speak to Tomika Sanders again! Tomika sat up stiff as a board when Mrs. Carter called her name. But unlike me, Tomika always blew these kinds of things off. She never worried about getting in trouble because she knew her Mom wasn't going to punish her. Most of the time, her mom defended her behavior. But my Mama would stomp my behind if I got in trouble in school!

I remember one time I got an infraction because of, as the note stated, "excessive talking." Once a teacher wrote you up, your parents had to sign the infraction and send it back.

Of course, I wasn't about to show my parents the infraction and miss my favorite T.V. shows or seeing the light of day after school for who knows how long. So I did what any normal kid would do. I hid it in my pants and decided I would later sign it myself. When I got home that afternoon, my friend Barbara stopped by to show me her new bike. I was excited because this meant I didn't have to peddle her on my handlebars anymore. We both jumped on our bikes and rode all over the neighborhood, stopping here and there, showing off to friends. We played so hard that day, I forgot to empty my pockets before throwing my pants in the laundry basket. Little did I know, Mama would be washing clothes that night. And what did she find in the pocket of my pants? You guessed it, a crinkled but readable pink infraction. Worst punishment to this day!

Mrs. Carter stood impatiently at the head of the class waiting for an answer. I felt like all eyes were on me, especially Herman's. Now he'd know me alright. He'd know me as the goofy seventh grader that got chewed out by Mrs. Carter. I lowered my head as Mrs. Carter continued speaking. I didn't dare look Tomika's way for the rest of the period.

"Does everyone understand the assignment?" asked Mrs. Carter in her New York accent. She always spoke as if she was speaking in a Shakespearian plays on Broadway. Vincent raised his hand.

"Yes, young man," said Mrs. Carter.

"How long does the paper have to be?" he asked.

Paper! What paper? We have to write a paper? Did I just miss the assignment?

"I would like at least two pages. Skip a line in between sentences please," commanded Mrs. Carter. Moans filled the room. "However, since it is getting close to the end of the six weeks, and we have a couple of test next week, I'll let you slide with a page and a half. But, if you choose to write fewer words, they better be meaningful. Am I clear?"

Like a chorus, the class replied, "Yes, Mrs. Carter."

The bell rung and I couldn't have been more relieved to leave the room. I wanted to stop by Mrs. Carter's desk to ask for the assignment again but I was too afraid of getting embarrassed a second time for not listening to the instructions. I would just have to get it from one of my classmates. I sure wasn't gonna ask Tomika. She was the reason I missed the assignment in the first place. I waited until Herman left the room with his friends before walking out the door. Tomika was waiting on the outside against the wall.

"I'm sorry Stacy," she said, but I could tell from the grin on her face that wasn't totally true. "I didn't mean to get you in trouble. I was just teasing," she added.

"It's not funny, Tomika. I got embarrassed in front of the whole class and I missed the assignment," I said.

"Girl, don't worry about that. She just wants us to write a paper on what we think beauty means," Tomika said as we walked down the busy hall.

"Why does she want us to write about beauty?" I asked.

"Because of the poets we've been talking about this week. They wrote about beauty and now she wants us to do the same. Boy, you haven't been listening to anything. You're too busy thinking about Herman," Tomika teased.

"No, that's not it! How could I listen with you making faces at me? When is it due?" I said.

"Not until Friday and you know I was just playing. Anyway, there's my bus. I gotta go. Call me tonight. Oh, wait. Here's my new number. I forgot to tell you we got it changed yesterday."

"Why?"

"I don't know. Something about bills."

Tomika quickly scribbled her number on a piece of paper then took off for the bus, waving good-bye. I know I should have kept my vow never to speak to her again, but Tomika always had a way of making the very thing I was upset about not seem like a big deal. Maybe that's why her mom found it hard to ground her.

I walked to my locker with my mind stuck on sixth period. Boy, was I glad school was over. I laid my folder on the top shelf and pulled specific textbooks from the messy locker. After stuffing my book bag, I closed the door and headed toward the front of the school, not realizing I had just left Tomika's number behind. As I walked to the doors, a boy I didn't recognize stepped in front of me, blocking my path. I could tell he was an eighth grader by his size. Tall and bulky like a football player. He stared at me with a silly expression.

"Are you Stacy Bell?" he asked.

"Yes."

"Here. This for you," he said as he handed me a small folded note, then took off down the hall as if he had just made me the "It" in a game of Tag. I started to yell after him but I was more curious about knowing what was in the note than knowing *his* name. Did Tomika spill the beans to Herman behind my back? The more I thought about it, the more my knee started bouncing back and forth.

Chapter Three

I stood on the steps in front of the school waiting for Granny to arrive. I held tightly to the folded note. Many thoughts raced through my mind. Was it a note from Herman saying he wanted to meet me? Or was the note telling me his feelings weren't the same as mine? If it was from Herman, I wondered why he sent someone else to make the delivery. Did the boy who gave me the note know about the secret too?

There were too many questions to think about so I decided to just open it and get it over with. One thing's for sure, whoever folded the note wanted to make sure no one but me could read its contents. It was like matching the colors on a Rubik's Cube just to get it open. I was almost to the end of the maze when I heard a familiar car horn. It was Granny honking. Three thirty, right on time. I quickly folded the note in half, stuffed it in my pocket, gathered my book bag and crossed the dead grass to the car. Granny greeted me with an, "I'm so proud of you" smile as I closed the door.

"Hello love. How was school?" she asked.

"It was okay," I said. Then it hit me! Granny could press my hair with the hot comb! It may not be a Golden Girl perm but this way, I wouldn't have to bug Mama and get asked a bunch of suspicious questions. Besides, Granny could straighten hair a little better than Mama, and she didn't pull as hard. I was what my family called "tender-headed". That meant, it didn't matter how soft Mama tried to comb my hair, I would still flinch and howl as if she was plucking my hair out, strand by strand.

"Granny?" I said.

"Yes baby?" she answered as she leaned closer to the steering wheel, peering out the window like a scientist looking down a microscope.

"Are you staying at our house for a little while?" I asked.

"Not tonight, honey. I gotta go to church. We got a guest speaker this evening from Chicago and I want to be in the front row. You know you got to get to these services early if you want to be front row. Plus, Brother Scott is singing in the choir. He's my favorite. If you finish your homework on time and ya Mama says it's okay, I'll swing by and pick you up. Pastor always enjoys seeing you," she said.

My eyes grew wide and before I knew it, I yelled a big fat "No!" I had some serious plans for the evening and letting Pastor pinch my cheeks wasn't on my 'To Do' list. I'd have to save that activity for Sunday. Although, I did need God's help right now. Perhaps a longer goodnight prayer before bed would make up for not going to church with Granny.

For a split second, Granny took her focus off the road and looked at me surprised.

"Well now. Why you answer like that?" she asked. I covered up my nervousness by laughing.

"I'm just playing Granny. I like the choir too, but I got a lot of homework," I said. Granny cracked a mini smile and returned to being the watchdog of the road.

I blew a sigh of relief and went back to plotting Operation Beauty Makeover. How was I gonna get Mama to perm my hair? *Rule #21: Straightening hair is for special occasions.* Not for being introduced to a boy. I couldn't say it was picture day because we'd already taken school pictures. Awards day was at the end of the year, and it certainly wasn't Easter. This was going to take some serious planning. I only had one night to transform from nerd to one of the coolest seventh graders at Forrest Hill Middle School.

But first, I was dying to see what was in that letter burning a whole in my pocket! I started to take it out but I knew I wouldn't be able to read in peace with Granny in the car. She would only interrupt me with questions about school. I decided to wait until I had total privacy behind the locked door of my room.

Granny spoke about people I didn't know all the way home. In a way, I was scared to get out of the car. Things would be different if Granny was staying. Asking Mama in front of Granny would make my plan easier. Granny might be able to convince Mama if she were to say no.

"Granny you coming in?" I asked with my best smile.

"Oh no, baby. I got to do something to my hair. It's going take awhile and you know I want to be early," she said as she kept the car running.

"Well Granny, I was hoping you could straighten my hair this afternoon. You see there's an event going on at school, and I really want to look nice for it," I said in my best granddaughter voice.

"Why don't you ask your Mama? I'm sure she wouldn't mind doing something cute to your head," Granny said.

"She might come home late tonight and if she does, she might be too tired to fix my hair. Besides Granny, you do a much better job. She pulls my hair too tight. Please Granny, please?"

"Oh honey, Granny wishes she could help but I just got too many things to do before church. I gotta whip up something for the reception and I have to fix my own hair. I'm sorry baby. Maybe your Mama won't be home late tonight. Either way, I'm sure you'll look pretty for tomorrow. You always do," said Granny.

I felt another blow to the head. This was becoming harder than I thought.

"Tell your Mama I'll call tonight to tell her about church. Don't slam the door," Granny warned. Don't slam the door? I felt she was the one slamming the door on me. Gently, I closed the door and watched the car burn rubber down the street.

After Granny's car was out of view, I turned toward the house. Dad's truck was parked in the driveway. Why couldn't *he* know how to do hair?

I walked in the house and right away heard the sounds of my brothers fighting over video games. I tossed my book bag and jacket on the dining room table and headed straight to the kitchen. One can't think on an empty stomach. As I closed the refrigerator door with an arm full of ingredients for a sandwich, my brother Derrick, an 8-year-old gnat, jumped up and yelled a loud roar, almost causing me to drop the food. Of course, he found his prank to be funny.

Derrick was tall like Dad. People always thought he was older than his actual age because of his height and size. He was also in that funny-looking stage when your teeth and nose are bigger than your face. But even though he had over-sized body parts, I could tell he was going to be okay looking when he got older because he had Dad's, as older women say, handsome smile and Mama's almond shaped eyes.

"You so silly Derrick!" I yelled.

"Gotcha!" he proudly yelled back. I tried to take a swing at him but he dodged my blow in time.

"Missed me!" Derrick taunted as he ran off to the living room.

I was so mad my punch didn't land on his chubby arm that I changed my mind about the sandwich. A handful of cookies would have to do. There was no more time to waste. I grabbed my things and headed upstairs to my room. Lost in thought, I passed my parents' bedroom without noticing Dad. We usually talked a little about school before I started my homework. Sometimes he would help me work through my assignments faster so we could play a quick game of one-on-one before it got dark. But this time I would have to take a rain check on the game. Today was all about the transformation from an unknown to a Superstar!

Before the change could begin, I just had to know what was in the note. I jerked it out of my pocket so hard, the material from inside stuck out like rabbit ears from my jacket. I stood in the middle of the room with one knee bouncing back and forth, reading each word as if it was one of those state practice tests. It was becoming quite clear this was serious. It read:

YOU KNOW ME AND I KNOW YOU.

BUT YOU DON'T KNOW I LIKE YOU TOO.

YOUR SECRET ADMIRER

My mouth dropped open when I got to the end. That so-call-friend Tomika must've told Herman behind my back! Why else would an eighth grader give *me* a note? Oh my goodness! I was upset, nervous and excited all at the same time. I didn't like that Tomika jumped ahead of our plans, but I was thrilled to know Herman had the same feelings!

I carefully folded the note and placed it back in my jacket. It was time to get down to business and wardrobe was first on the list. I opened the closet door and sifted back and forth through the thin line of clothes. The more I searched, the more disappointed I became. Was there anything I hadn't worn yet? Why couldn't I get a new outfit every week like Tomika or have an older sister who would let me borrow her clothes?

As I shoved cookie after cookie in my mouth, I became frustrated over the combination of clothes lying on the bed. The colors of my shirts were faded from countless washings, my pants sagged in all the wrong places and my skirts stopped below my knees which made me look like I went to one of those strict Catholic schools you'd see in the movies. In 1983, miniskirts were in style, but, like always, Mama had some excuse why she wasn't buying the latest trends. Her excuse this time was, she refused to buy anything that might show my underwear whenever I sat down. It was hopeless, so I took a break from fashion and went to the bathroom to try some new hairstyles.

I stood in front of the mirror and sighed. My hair fell just above my shoulders. Brown and thick just like cold chocolate frosting. I took the rubber bands out and brushed my hair gently, being careful not to hurt my tender head. I began positioning my hair in different styles. In a ponytail on top of my head like a genie, half of it pulled up into a ponytail with the rest down in the back or all of it down, placing the part on the side instead of in the middle.

Wearing my hair down was going to be another hurdle to jump. This was another style Mama didn't allow. *Rule #40: Stacy is not allowed to wear all of her hair down until high school.* Mama felt each age had its own privileges and thirteen was not old enough to look fifteen. This left me with another challenge of convincing Mama to break *this* rule a few years early.

As I worked on my hair, Dad stepped in the doorway. He still had on his crisp, starched uniform pants from the post office and a white T-shirt. His tall, broad figure in the doorway made the frame look small enough to fit a children's playhouse. The light from the bathroom shined on the top of his bald head.

"There you are. I thought I heard you come in. How come you didn't say hello?" said Dad. I stopped combing and gave him a hug.

"Hi Daddy. Sorry about that."

"What you getting all dolled up for? You going somewhere?" Dad asked as he tickled my sides.

"No," I said, laughing.

"Get out of the mirror and come play some basketball with me. Your brothers are stuck on that game so they're out."

"I can't today Daddy." He looked surprised.

"No playing with Daddy today?"

"I kinda got some stuff to do," I mumbled. I felt a little bad about turning him down. I knew how much he liked playing basketball. You could hear him all the way down the block, cheering himself on when he made a basket. Basketball season was a big deal in our family and our house was the meeting place for all his friends to watch the games.

I liked when Dad's friends came over. They were funny, especially when they started playing The Dozens. Their outbursts of laughter from this playful game bounced off the walls of our home like a ping-pong ball. The Dozens was when one person joked about the faults of another person or his family, but the standing rule of the game was you never took what was said seriously. My Dad was the king when it came to this game. He would have everyone laughing, including the person he was ragging on. Sometimes, I'd laugh so hard, I thought I would wet my pants.

Though I knew Dad was disappointed that none of his children wanted to play a friendly game of basketball, he took it well.

"That's okay. Anything I can help you with?" he asked.

"Can you put a perm on my hair?"

He looked at me confused. "Not likely," he said, laughing at the thought of combing my hair. He kissed me on the forehead and walked down the hall. Oh well, it was worth a shot.

After Dad left I heard a car door close. I rushed over to the window and peeked out. It was Mama. The moment had arrived and I still wasn't sure of what to say. I quickly brushed my hair into one ponytail and took a deep breath. If God wasn't angry at me for not going to church with Granny, maybe He would help me convince Mama to bend her rules for one night.

Chapter Four

Mama stumbled into the kitchen from the garage with an arm full of groceries. Barely making it through the door, she stopped and called for my brothers to rescue the bags that were slowly slipping from her grip. But beeping electronic noises from the video game rose above Mama's cry for help. Growing impatient, she belted out their names as loud as her voice allowed. The call of their names traveled from the kitchen to the living room, clashing with the electronic sounds of Pac Man. Finally, the ringing of Mama's voice in their ears caused them to quickly stand to attention. I could hear their feet running into the kitchen.

"Grab these bags," Mama demanded. When they realized this was their only punishment for not responding on her first call, they anxiously grabbed the bags, threw them on the counter and started off toward the living room to complete level four. "Hold it you two," Mama said as she stood up straight and blew out a sigh of relief. "Have you done your homework?" she asked with a stern voice. Frozen in their tracks, my brothers looked at each other trying to figure out who would handle the question. My youngest brother, Dean, volunteered to be first. Even though he was the youngest, Dean never had a problem saying what was on his mind. Unlike Derrick, Dean was small and lean. He got that from Mama's Dad, Grandpa Ray. His body reminded me of the stick people I use to draw in kindergarten. Dean and I looked more alike because of our looks favoring Mama.

She was short, and at one time, very skinny. That was before she had me. She often complained about the weight she gained after having kids and always told us to be ready because she was going to be giving *our* weight back any day. Her skin was a honey brown complexion and for most of my childhood, she wore her hair brushed back into a tight ponytail. She would wrap the ponytail into a small bun that sat on the back of her head. Nothing fancy, just professional.

"Derrick has more homework than me Mama! I'm only six," said Dean. Derrick looked surprised when his partner in crime played innocent.

"Uh-uh Mama!" Derrick said.

"Yes you do!" argued Dean.

"Alright you two, that's enough. The answer to my question must be no, so cut that T.V. off and go upstairs to your room and start your homework. I *will* be checking it so make sure it's neat," Mama said while she began putting away the food. As they headed back to the living room, Derrick snuck a punch on Dean's skinny little arm. The small tit-for-tat lead to a shoving match. I would have enjoyed ratting out this daily fight but I was too nervous to concentrate on them. I took a deep breath and put a frozen smile on my face as I entered the kitchen.

"Hi Mama! How was your day?"

"Busy. How was yours?" asked Mama without stopping her task. Everything had its place in her kitchen. *Rule # 28: If you take something out, put it back where it belongs.* Watching her put away the groceries was like watching a robot. She moved in a fast pace like a one-woman factory. Mama always thought order made life simpler.

"Oh, you know. Same old stuff. Do you need some help?" I said in my most pleasant voice. Mama instantly flipped the switch to OFF in the factory and stared at someone who looked like her daughter but wasn't acting like her daughter. Never did her children volunteer their help. She usually had to drag out of us.

"That would be nice," Mama said. She smiled as if she had just hired a new employee in her one-woman factory and began a new task of folding the sacks, although, she turned her head toward me suspiciously.

"What happened to your hair?" said Mama.

"Oh, I was just playing with it in the bathroom," I said. I began putting the food away while Mama folded the last sack. Finished with her task, she sat down at the kitchen table and plopped her feet up in a chair. I made sure not to mess up the order of the food pantry such as mixing canned tomatoes with the afternoon snacks. As I carefully put away the groceries, I thought now would be a good time to ask since she seemed relaxed. *Remember,* I reminded myself, *don't sound too eager and don't trip over your words.* Mama always said tripping over your words meant you were trying to make up a story. *Rule #5: Always tell the truth, no matter the consequences.*

"Mama," I said. Her eyes were closed as she answered with a moan. "I was wondering if we could go to the store and buy a Golden Girl perm for my hair?" Mama slightly lifted her head and opened her eyes.

"When?"

"Tonight?" I said, avoiding eye contact.

"Perm your hair? Tonight? What for?"

"For school pictures." I finished unloading the last bag and took another big breath, trying to slow down the rhythm of my heart.

"I thought you already took pictures this year?" Mama asked. I kept my distance by staying at the counter. I didn't want to stand too close for fear she might have been able to sniff out the lie.

"Yes, but some of the students' pictures didn't develop so we have to retake them tomorrow."

"Why didn't I get a letter about this? And why do you need a perm to re-take a picture? You didn't have one the first time," said Mama. Uh-oh. I didn't prepare for these questions. Nothing was coming to mind; just blank space. Finally, I stuttered an answer.

"Well they're putting our pictures in the yearbook and I just wanted to look really good," I said. It was the best I could do on short notice. Mama looked puzzled. She didn't seem to be buying my story. I stood as stiff as the toast they served at school for breakfast, waiting for an answer.

"Well, I don't know why this is the first time I'm hearing about it, but I'm not going to perm your hair tonight. I'm braiding it," she said while thumbing through the mail on the table. What! Did she say braiding? Maybe I misunderstood her. I mean, I *was* standing a few feet from her chair.

"You're braiding my hair?" I asked, as my voice almost trailed off to a whisper. Mama wasn't paying attention to my crumbling body when she simply answered, "Yes."

This couldn't be happening. I was facing the most important day of my seventh grade year and my Mama was about to ruin EVERYTHING! I mean, there was a note in my room from the boy of my dreams for goodness sakes! Tomorrow could change my school image forever and Mama wanted to put braids in my hair? Braids weren't cool, at least not where I lived. In my town, girls at school wore their hair in two styles; a Jheri Curl or permed. That's it! Braids were considered cute in the fifth grade, not the seventh. Even Michael Jackson had a Jheri Curl! Was she trying to ruin my rep on purpose? I felt as though someone had just punched me in the stomach. I walked over to Mama trying to stay calm, but my heart pumped overtime as I approached her. I could feel the heat simmering on my face.

"Mama, please don't braid my hair. I don't like braids," I said. Mama looked at me surprised.

"What do you mean you don't like braids? You use to beg me to put braids in your hair."

"That was in elementary. I'm in middle school now and nobody wears braids," I whined.

"Oh Stacy, you're making a big deal out of nothing. Braids don't go out of style. They can be worn anytime in *any* grade. Besides, I'll be leaving for work early and coming home late for the rest of this week. We have a big project to finish and I'm in charge so I won't have time to oversee your hair. And your father doesn't know a thing about styles. He'll let you go to school looking like you just woke up. This way, all you'll have to do is get dressed and I will have peace of mind knowing your hair is presentable."

"Mama please! It will take too long. We'll be up all night! I have to start on my English paper," I pleaded.

"Well, quit wasting time talking about it and get started while I cook dinner. Besides, perming your thick head of hair will take just as long, if not longer. What's the difference? Either way, you'll look nice for the pictures tomorrow if that's what you're whining about," Mama said as she got up to go upstairs.

"I don't want to take pictures with braids. Braids are ugly!" I shouted. The words came out in desperation before I could think. Mama turned around, with her lips pressed firmly together.

"You listen to me little girl. I don't ever put anything on you, or anyone else in this family, that is ugly. I happen to think you look beautiful in braids. But for some reason, you seem to be making a very big deal about this whole hair situation. Why?" asked Mama as she shoved her arms in a folding position across her chest.

"I don't know. I just wanted my hair permed," I mumbled, staring at the floor.

"Well, that's not going to happen tonight. I'm a little tired from today and at least I can sit down while braiding your hair," she said in a lower tone. "Now, I suggest you get started on your homework. Maybe you'll be done by the time I start on your hair," she said. Before leaving, took one last look at my disappointed face. "And Stacy, nothing about you is ugly."

With that said, Mama walked upstairs. I stood in the kitchen feeling hopeless. What had the potential to be a wonderful day would soon turn into a disaster. The only thing left to do was to call Tomika and tell her the meeting was off.

I went upstairs and looked in my book bag but couldn't find the piece of paper with her new phone number. I dumped everything out on the bed and still couldn't find it. I retraced my steps in my mind and in a panic, suddenly remembered I had put it on the top shelf of my locker. That's where I must have left it! How could I have been so forgetful? As I stared at the floor in disbelief, rocking my leg back and forth, I thought to myself, could this get any worse?

Chapter Five

I was quiet throughout dinner. My mind was working over-time, trying to figure out how I was going to get to Tomika tomorrow morning before she brought Herman over. But then, how was I gonna stop Herman from talking to me? After writing that note, he was bound to say *something* to me. I knew I should have kept my big mouth shut. If I'da just stayed in my dreams, I wouldn't have to worry about any of this. *Rule #30: Don't tell your business to everyone. Some things are better left unsaid.* Being a nobody was looking better every minute. The only wise choice would be to deny any and everything Tomika might have said to Herman. And who knows, I thought, maybe Mama won't do my entire head. Maybe she'll just braid the front. If it had to be braided, I'd take half a head!

"Stacy," Mama said breaking my thoughts. "Hurry up and finish your food so I can get started on your hair. We're gonna be up late enough. Did you finish your paper?

"Almost," I mumbled.

"When is it due?" she asked as she carefully scooped a fork full of sweet peas in her mouth.

"Friday," I said while strategically trying to hide my peas under mounds of mashed potatoes. Nobody but Mama really liked sweet peas. Daddy just ate them to be an example for us kids. But he too left a few wrinkled green monsters on his plate at the end of dinner.

"Well, your Dad can help you finish it tomorrow since I will be working late," Mama said as she started clearing the table.

"Mama, will you braid half of my hair and leave the rest down in the back? I'm really tired," I asked.

"No Stacy. I'm braiding all of it," Mama said without a pause. She had turned on the ON switch and began arranging things back in order. "I don't want you wasting anytime in the morning messin' with your hair."

"Why don't you let Daddy do her hair in the morning Mama?" Derrick said laughing at his own joke. He was the clown of the house and was always willing to tell a joke at the wrong time. I cut my eyes at him, wanting to punch him in the arm. Daddy, jumping on the funny wagon, added his dry humor.

"Why look so down about the idea of me doing your hair? Might not be so bad," he said trying to finish his sentence without laughing. Everyone was becoming a comedian. "I'm sorry honey. Daddy doesn't mean to tease you," he said as he stood to clear his area. He pushed his scraps of food in the trash and grabbed two chocolate chip cookies as he left the kitchen. Derrick and Dean scurried from the table in an attempt to dump their plates in the sink, polluting the lemon-fresh dishwater with a few green pea monsters. Mama caught them before the plates touched her water.

"Hold it you two. Empty your plates on the other side of the sink. You know I don't like food floating around in my dishwater," Mama demanded. Their forks scraping against the plates sounded like someone's nails sliding down a chalkboard. I could tell it bothered Mama as she pressed her lips together while supervising. However, Derrick and Dean were too worried about playing one more video game before bath and bed to be bothered by her aggravated expression. I emptied my plate after my brothers finished without saying a word. What was the use? There weren't any more plans to be made. Couldn't call Tomika, couldn't get half a head of braids and couldn't look pretty for one important day. Just wave the ugly wand over my head and get it over with. After wiping down the table, I headed toward my room.

"Hurry up and take your shower Stacy," said Mama. She was too busy washing dishes to notice my pitiful expression.

After showering, I walked down the steps wearing my favorite football jersey that came past my knees, and carrying a pillow to sit on. I tried to wear the saddest face I could find. Maybe Mama would have sympathy and cancel the whole beauty appointment. But when I turned the corner to enter the living room, things got worse! The sight of it stopped me in my tracks. My heart began to beat faster and faster as I approached the couch. Mama was busy setting up shop with comb, brush, Blue Magic grease and, Heaven help us, BEADS! Please... not beads! Beads are cute when you're five or seven. After that, it's history. *Dear God, please whisper to Mama and tell her nobody wears beads anymore!*

"Sit down Stacy," Mama said arranging the hair tools. I guess He was busy.

"I don't want beads in my hair, Mama," I pleaded.

"Why not? It's going to look so pretty," said Mama.

"Nobody wears beads," I said.

"Oh Stacy, there you go again with that "what's not in" talk. Who cares what people think?" *Rule #28: It's not what others think of you that matters; it's what you think of yourself.*

"I told you, braids and beads never go out of style. Now sit down," she ordered. It was clear Mama was running out of patience. I placed the pillow between Mama's legs and plopped down. As the combed pulled through the stiff thick tresses, my shoulders flinched up and down to pacify the pain. This was going to be a long night. And in the end, I was not turning into a swan as I had hoped. I was turning into a duck...with beads.

Chapter Six

The air seemed cooler the next morning as it blew on my exposed scalp. In Mama's mind, my hair was a beautiful arrangement of lines crisscrossed around my head with small beads of color that hung like tiny ornaments on a Christmas tree. But to me, it was a crown of shame.

"Alright honey. Have a good day at school," Dad said as the car idled by the curb. I just sat in the car looking out the window. I couldn't move. The thought of what was about to happen scared me to death. Why couldn't I get sick? Why couldn't the school have mysteriously burnt down the night before?

Dad looked at me, puzzled. "You getting out?" he asked with a smile. I remained quiet. "Something wrong Stacy?" I was about to answer when I saw more buses than usual arriving at the same time. That meant some of them must have been running behind. It also meant Tomika's *and* Herman's buses were arriving together, leaving no time to talk to Tomika before the meeting. I would just have to find Tomika in the hallway before class and explain what happened.

I grabbed my backpack and reached on the floor of the car where I thought I had placed my knit hat. I was planning on wearing it all day as a cover up. I ran my hand underneath my seat and was relieved when I felt a piece of material. RATS! It was my brother's missing glove. I threw my body over the back seat, scanning every corner. No hat.

"What are you looking for?" asked Dad.

"My hat! I had my hat with me when we left the house!" I said in a panic.

"Is it brown and white?" he asked.

"Yeah! You have it?"

"No. I saw it on the kitchen counter. You must have left it there," said Dad.

I flipped around and sank into the seat in total disbelief. How could I have left something so important *again*? First, I left Tomika's number in my locker and now this? Where was my mind when I needed it? I looked out the window once more and saw the students exiting the buses. "Dad, can you drive further up the street?" I asked. Dad began letting out big puffs of air.

"Stacy, I'm running late. What is this all about?" he asked. I figure I better get out of the car right then before I'd have to explain.

"Nothing. Gotta go Daddy! See ya." Before he could ask more questions, I jumped out of the car. As Dad drove off, I made a dash across the schoolyard, but was cut off by a familiar voice.

"Stacy?" said Tomika. She looked shocked by what she saw. I stopped in my steps and slowly turned around. Tomika's eyes grew big. "What…did…you…do…to…your…hair?"

"I didn't do this. You think I can do this? My Mama did this."

"I thought you were getting a perm," said Tomika.

"I tried to get her to straighten it, but she wouldn't listen."

"Well, do you still want to meet Herman?" Tomika asked, turning her nose as if she smelled something bad.

"No! And I thought you said you wouldn't say anything to him before today!"

"I didn't," said Tomika.

"Then why did a boy give me this note yesterday?" I pulled the note from my pocket and handed it to Tomika. She snatched the note from my hand and opened it like it was her report card. As she read, her mouth hung open, growing wider with each sentence.

"Who gave this to you?" she asked.

"I don't know his name. He just walked up to me after you left and asked if I was Stacy Bell. I said yes, then he gave me this note and ran off," I explained.

"Well, I don't know who this is, but I promise I didn't say a word to Herman about you liking him. I just said I wanted him to meet a friend when he came over to play with my brother yesterday," Tomika said.

"Tomika! You messed it up! Now he's really gonna know I like him," I barked.

"I was just doing what you asked me to do. You should've called and told me you didn't want to meet him anymore," Tomika fired back.

"I left your number in my locker," I said, staring at the plain, lifeless building we called our school. I couldn't look at Tomika because I knew she was right. It was my fault she didn't know. Everything was my fault. We both remained quiet a few seconds.

"Well, I don't know what you're mad about. Evidently he likes you or he wouldn't have written the note," said Tomika. I could tell from the tone of her voice, she was trying to make me feel better.

She did have a point. Maybe I was blowing things up. But still, I wasn't sure about meeting him so I decided just to call the whole thing off. At that point, I saw Herman and his posse heading our way.

"I change my mind. I don't want to meet Herman. Quick, he's coming this way! Let's go to the cafeteria before he sees us," I said.

We started to walk away until a tall figure crossed our path, blocking our escape. It was Herman, standing in unwelcomed territory with his posse a few feet behind. For the first time, he was the last person I wanted to see.

Light from the bright morning sun reflected in his face causing him to squint his dreamy hazel-green eyes. He exposed a slight grin that made me wonder if Tomika really did say more than she admitted. His body leaned to one side due to the heavy book bag resting on his hip and the scent of glycerin mixed with Old Spice deodorant filled my nose, making my knees weak. *Please God, just open the ground so I can disappear.* Common sense would have told me to keep walking toward the cafeteria, but I couldn't move. I stood still with my head hung low, staring at my dusty shoes.

"Hey Tomika," he said with ease. He was one of three boys out of the whole eighth grade class whose voice had already cracked. It had a soft baritone sound, like the tuba section in our marching band. Hearing him always gave me butterflies in my stomach. But at that moment, I could have lived without hearing his voice.

Tomika looked as if she had been caught in big lie. She mumbled hello while staring in the opposite direction. Herman remained quiet as if he was waiting to be formally introduced. When no one spoke up, he asked the dreaded question; "This your friend?" I could feel Tomika looking at me, waiting for me to say something. I couldn't. My jaws were sealed shut like a mouth full of taffy.

"Uh, huh. This my friend Stacy. Stacy, this is Herman," Tomika said, barely looking at us. She seemed more embarrassed than I was. Barely raising my head, I managed to utter "hello" back to him. It was then that I caught a glimpse of his face. He didn't have to say anything. I could tell from his frown, he wasn't too pleased by the sight of me. My heart began to pound as I shuffled the dirt under my shoe from one foot to the other. I was going to be the joke of the day for sure now. For a minute, we were all silent. Finally, Herman spoke again.

"Well, I gotta go. Tomika, tell Kasey to meet me on the courts after school."

"Okay," she said. She blew out her words as if she had been holding her breath.

My nose became extra moist and I blinked more times than usual to hold back the tears forming in my eyes. Tomika gave me a small shove on my arm. It was her way of snapping me out of self-pity.

"Don't worry about that, girl. He like you. He's just being shy," she said. *Yeah right*, I thought to myself.

"I should have never told you," I mumbled.

"What you getting mad at me for?"

"I'm not mad at you. I just wish I'd never said anything about liking Herman. Then I never would have been talked into meeting him," I said.

Truth is, I really was mad at Tomika. And, I was mad at Herman for the look he gave me. But most of all, I was mad at Mama for having too many rules about hair. *Rule #60: No hair dying until age eighteen.*

I wondered if other girls had as many hair rules as I did. Tomika could never understand my frustrations because she had a Curl. Things always worked out for her. Sometimes I wondered how we stayed friends so long.

We both said nothing as the bell rang for school. Every step I took felt as though all eyes were on me. The sounds of snickering as I walked down the hall followed me like a shadow. I don't know if I was the reason for their laughter, but it sure felt like it. I wanted to cry but instead held it in. I just wanted to get through the day without anyone saying anything about my hair, then go home and bury my head under my pillow. My seventh grade year was ruined, and to top it off, meeting Herman Price was the most embarrassing day of my life!

Chapter Seven

It was Dad's turn to pick us up from school. I was quiet during the ride home. My brothers were in the back seat making noises with their body parts. Most days this would bother me, but I was lost in my thoughts. Dad hadn't noticed my silence or the sounds coming from the back seat. Like me, he was too lost in his own world, singing to the oldies on his favorite radio station.

What a day it had been. I got the worse case of embarrassment a girl could ever get from meeting a boy, got a low score on Mr. Boyd's pop quiz in Math, and I lost my lunch money but didn't know it until I reached Mrs. Lovett, the cashier. I searched all of my pockets, but kept coming up with lint. "I had it. I really did!" I declared. Mrs. Lovett frowned, displeased that I was holding up her line.

"You must pay what you owe by tomorrow or you won't be able to eat!" she'd shouted in her raspy voice. Gee whiz! Did she have to announce it to the whole cafeteria? To top it off, Herman never said another word to me all day. Then again, I was glad he didn't bother. I wouldn't have known what to say. Nobody made a comment about my hair but there was no need. Their stares said everything. The girls in gym stared at me like I was the nerd of the century. Even Tomika acted as if I let *her* down. She talked to other kids more than me. She even talked to kids who weren't her friends! Was this the end of our friendship? I mean, we've had disagreements before like, which rapper was better looking or who owes who in a game of Monopoly, even homework problems, but never to the point of us hardly speaking to each other.

When we were in the sixth grade, Tomika always stood up for me when I wouldn't do it for myself. Most of the time, I tried to avoid trouble by ignoring the potential beat down. But not Tomika. She would step to anyone who picked on me. Her favorite line was, *I bet you won't say that to me.* When most kids heard that, they'd back off because nobody wanted to be on Tomika's bad side. It made me feel good knowing she was willing to be my bodyguard. With all the fights she saved me from, surely a hairstyle wouldn't come between us. Maybe tomorrow would be different. Perhaps everyone, including Tomika, will be over the shock of my out-of-style cornrows and speak to me as if nothing was wrong.

"Whew!" Dad shouted, interrupting my thoughts. "That was my song when I was a young man," he said. Here comes the "I remember when" story. Sure enough, he started to narrate a tall tale that lasted until we turned into the driveway. Getting out of the car was a relief. Usually I was a good listener because his stories were funny. I just wasn't in the mood to laugh.

I walked to the mailbox to get the mail while my brothers chased each other around in circles in the front yard. I walked past them and stood behind Dad as he fumbled with the keys, still singing his favorite song. Dad held the open the door and as I entered, I could feel him staring at my hair. "Wow Stacy. Your Mama really went all out on your hair this time. It looks pretty, honey. I meant to tell you that this morning but you jumped out of the car so fast. I bet you were the talk of the school today!" he proudly said. *You have no clue,* I said as I laid my books on the dining room table.

I went to the kitchen to get something to eat and saw a note taped to the refrigerator door. It was from Mama. In it was the menu for dinner and everyone's assigned chores, including Dad. I started to make a peanut butter and jelly sandwich for myself but I knew if my brothers saw my eating, they would whine to Dad. I wasn't in the mood for a fight so I made the crybabies sandwiches too. When the table was set, I called them into the kitchen. As usual, they entered with a lot of noise.

"Sit down and cut out all that hollering," I shouted.

"Stop yelling at me. You not the Mama," Dean yelled back.

"You see this letter? This is from Mama telling me *I'm* in charge, so you have to do what *I* say."

"I bet you won't say that to Daddy," Derrick said with a mouth full of sandwich. Just when I was about to issue another threat, Dad walked into the kitchen.

"Why is everyone yelling?" he asked.

"Tell him, Stacy. Tell Dad what you told us," Dean said wearing a big smile with breadcrumbs all over his face. I cut my eyes at him.

"Tell me what?" Dad said. I handed him the note. He mumbled the words as he raced through the memo then leaned back to release a hearty laughed. Shaking his head, he handed the note back to me and opened the pantry. "Your Mama is giving orders even when she's gone," he said. I took my sandwich and sat at the table only to find Dean staring at me with a crooked face.

"What are you looking at?" I asked.

"I'm trying to figure out which way your hair is going," Dean said. Derrick got a big kick out of his little brother's curiosity. They both laughed loud and long. I felt fire coming from my face. Even Dad laughed a little. It was hurtful to see him laugh. I thought he liked my hair.

"That's not funny!" I yelled to my brothers. But they didn't seem to care about my feelings. The joke was more important. Since I didn't see the humor in my hair, I decided to leave.

"Stacy, where you going?" Dad asked.

"Can I go to my room?" I asked in defiance.

"You don't want to finish your sandwich?" Dad asked.

"No sir." Dad dismissed me with a nod. When I entered my room, I plopped face down on the bed. I wanted to cry but was too upset. I was upset at myself for agreeing to meet Herman. What a stupid idea.

I was still upset at Mama for putting braids in my hair. I wished there was no such thing as braids. I took out a hand mirror from my bag, turned on my back and held it up to see myself. I was hoping to find something pretty but kept coming up with the Duck. I heard a knock at the door. I knew it was Dad from how soft his knuckles tapped against the door.

"Yes?" I called.

Dad walked in holding Dean and Derrick by their necks. All three of them stood with their heads low. "Your brothers have something to say," Dad said. They remained quiet until he put a little pressure on their necks, forcing them mumble the word "sorry."

"Go on now. Get to your schoolwork. No video games. I'll be there in a minute to help." Dad walked over to my bed and sat down. "I'm sorry for laughing cupcake. You know I like your hair."

"But you laughed," I said, pouting like a little girl

"I didn't mean nothing by it. I just got tickled at your brother," said Dad.

"That's alright. I know I look bad," I admitted. Dad leaned back, surprised.

"Wait a minute! Now who said that?" asked Dad.

"The whole school," I grunted as I turned on my side.

"Somebody made fun of you at school? Where they at?" he said while looking around the room. "I'll tear them up! I'll ..." Dad stopped putting on an act when he noticed my tears. I hadn't planned on crying but they came without control. "Hey, what's the tears for? Tell Daddy what's wrong."

"It's just that, I was expecting something good to happen today and nothing turned out right," I sobbed.

"Well, why are you sad about your hair?" asked Dad.

"This style wasn't part of the plan. Nobody wears their hair like this. Everybody laughed behind my back. Tomika barely talked to me today. I look ugly, and now I have to walk around like this for the next two weeks!" The disappointment and hurt rushed to the surface of my face so fast I hid my face in my hands. Dad put his arm around me and held on tight. He sat quietly for a minute. I guess he didn't know what to say. When he finally spoke, there was a serious tone to his voice.

"Look here baby girl. I'm really sorry for teasing you about your hair. I didn't know you were feeling this way. I think you look great. And I'm not just saying that because you're my daughter. I've always liked braids. You know, when I met your Mama, she was wearing braids," Dad said as if this would cheer me up.

"Dad, it was okay to wear them in the old days," I said. He did a small chuckle.

"The old days, huh? Well, I may not know what's in *these* days but I do know one thing. Your Mama didn't do this to punish you. If anybody was punished it was her. Do you know how much hair you've got? And look at all those itty-bitty beads across your head. Do you think she would go through all of that work to make you look ugly? I tell ya I couldn't do it. I'd have beads all over the floor," he said. I tried not to laugh because I knew that was his intention, but I couldn't help smiling a little.

"Don't pay attention to those kids at school and don't worry about Tomika. I have a feeling she's still your friend. I know what will cheer you up though," said Dad.

"What?" I said.

"Two words. Aunt Ruthy," he said. He was right. This did cheer me up. I loved being with my Aunt Ruthy because she played games with me and my brothers and let us eat stuff Mama didn't allow. "She's coming to pick you guys up and take you over to the community center. Would you like to go or are you still upset?" Dad teased.

"No Dad. I think I can go," I said.

"That's my girl," said Dad. He kissed me on the forehead, walked to the door and closed it behind him. I started to feel a little better. I was happy for Dad's talk and about Aunt Ruthy coming but I still had to face tomorrow. Herman Price now knew how I felt about him. I bet he told all the boys who hung on The Wall. Thinking about all the "what ifs" wasn't making things better, so I decided to concentrate on my English paper and the rest of my homework before Aunt Ruthy arrived. For the first time that day, I was looking forward to going somewhere.

Chapter Eight

I was finishing the end of my homework when I heard the doorbell ring. Immediately I stopped writing and sat up on my bed. When I heard Aunt Ruthy's voice, I jumped off and ran downstairs. There she was in a colorful floor length skirt with a matching headdress wrapped around her head like an African tiara. Her skirt reminded me of a Latin dancer's costume; full of bright colors woven together with thin threads of gold. Big hoop earrings dangled from her earlobes. She had a splash of red lipstick covering her mouth to match the red in her skirt. Her hands and neck were covered in Aztec rings, multiple bracelets and necklaces. She once told me her jewelry was made by descendants of the Aztec Indians. I didn't know if it was true, but it sure sounded interesting. She was always telling stories about different cultures. She said it was better to understand other people and their culture than to be prejudiced toward the unknown.

When I reached the end of the stairs, there she stood waiting by the door with her arms opened wide. I leaped off the last step and squeezed my arms around her small waist. She was still skinny like Mama used to be before she had us. Her dark-brown skin was scented with the sweet smell of cocoa butter lotion. It smelled like a chocolate factory. I liked hanging out with her because unlike Mama, Aunt Ruthy lived on the wild side!

"There's my Queen!" she shouted. "And how are you today?"

"Fine now," I said, grinning from ear-to-ear.

"Aren't you sweet. Where are my two Kings?" she said.

"Upstairs. Probably fooling around. I'll go get them," said Dad.

"So what are we gonna do at the center Aunt Ruthy? Paint?" I said.

"Not tonight. I'm teaching a different class. It's for girls only," she said.

"Good!" I replied, thankful not to have boys around. I'd had my share of embarrassments for the day. "What kinda class is it?" I asked.

"Oh, you're going to enjoy it. It's a class that allows girls to express themselves through theatre games, music and dance. We talk about girl stuff and learn about other cultures. We have a lot of fun," explained Aunt Ruthy. My brothers came running downstairs with all their noise. It seemed as though they could never do anything quietly.

"Aunt Ruthy!" they yelled.

"There are my Kings! Come give me a big hug," said Aunt Ruthy. They squeezed her tiny waist so hard she almost fell over.

"That's enough boys," Dad said as he pulled them apart. "You're gonna knock her down." She purposely kissed them hard on their cheeks to leave lip prints. Her laugh rolled out from deep within when they squinted their faces, trying to rub the red from their cheeks. I grabbed my jacket and headed for the car. Aunt Ruthy told Dad she'd have us back by seven. He waved good-bye and we were off.

"Stacy, who did your hair? It's so beautiful," said Aunt Ruthy.

"Mama," I said under my breath. The mention of my hair brought the mood down and brought back memories of the day's events. For a minute, I had forgotten what I looked like until Aunt Ruthy's comment. I know she didn't know how it would affect me, but after reminding me of my hair, going to the center didn't seem so exciting. I wanted to change my mind but I didn't want to disappoint Aunt Ruthy. "Hey, did I say something wrong?" Aunt Ruthy said as she closed the door. I shook my head no.

"She don't like her hair Auntie," said Dean.

"You shut your mouth Dean!" I snapped back.

"Whoa. Hold it you two. Dean, don't tease your sister. Is this true Stacy?" asked Aunt Ruthy. I nodded while looking out the passenger window, trying to prevent her from seeing my eyes welling up with tears. As Aunt Ruthy backed out the driveway, we were both silent. It seemed as though her mood had also changed. Only the sound of my brothers playing filled the car. I felt the need to apologize but I didn't know how to say it. Aunt Ruthy decided to break the silence for me.

"Did you have a bad day?" she asked.

I nodded.

"Do want to talk about it?"

"I'm not a little girl anymore but Mama doesn't think so," I said.

"Why do you say that?" asked Aunt Ruthy.

"Nobody wears their hair like this, but Mama didn't listen to me," I said. I was relieved to get it off my chest.

"You mean when she braided your hair?" asked Aunt Ruthy. I nodded. "Sometimes mothers find it hard to separate the little girl from the young woman. We love our daughters so much that we want them to stay sweet little girls forever. But as you know, that can't happen. Your mother loves you dearly. It's just hard to let go," said Aunt Ruthy.

I didn't know why Mama wanted me to stay a little girl. She was always reciting *Rule #53: When you graduate high school, your room will turn into my hobby room.* I had a bunch of unanswered questions spinning around in my head. Were Tomika and I still best friends? Who wrote the mystery note? Did I make a big deal over Herman's disappointed look?

"You know what Stacy? I think going to the center is going to help you forget about any troubles you had today. Just come in with an open mind and have as much fun as you can. You think you can do that for me?" asked Aunt Ruthy.

"Okay," I said with a smile. Aunt Ruthy always had a way of making sunshine out of a rainy day. At least, for a couple of hours.

Chapter Nine

When we pulled into the parking lot, almost every space was full. Gee whiz, I didn't count on *this* many people being at the center. I was starting to feel self-conscious about my hair again.

"Well now. The gang's all here!" Aunt Ruthy said as she pulled into an empty spot.

"Do we get to play basketball, Aunt Ruthy?" asked Dean.

"If we have time. But first, you guys get to go to an African drum class."

"Wow! Do we get to hit them?" asked Derrick.

"Of course you do!" said Aunt Ruthy. My brothers eagerly jumped out of the car, ready to go make more noise. Butterflies spiraled in circles in the pit of my stomach as I got out the car. Aunt Ruthy sensed my fear right away and put her arm around me. "Oh, it's not that bad. I promise, you'll feel better by the time we leave the center. Come on, I've got some young girls I want you to meet," Aunt Ruthy said.

When we walked into the center, it was full of activity. People behind the front desk were helping others, issuing basketballs or answering the telephone, which seemed to ring every two minutes. Kids of all ages were running in and out of different rooms so fast it looked like one of those practice fire drills we had at school.

"What's the fuss, Aunt Ruthy? Why is everybody running around?" I asked.

"They're trying to get to their classes on time. If you are punctual, the instructor gives you a treat," Aunt Ruthy explained.

"Can we go now, Aunt Ruthy? Can we go hit the drums?" asked my brothers.

"Yes my Kings, we can go. Stacy, why don't you have a seat on that bench over there while I walk your brothers to their room. I'll only be a minute," said Aunt Ruthy.

"Okay," I said.

The sounds of the drums were beginning to echo down the hall. My brothers pulled Aunt Ruthy by her arms as if *they* knew the way to the room. In a second, they disappeared around the corner. I walked over to the bench, sat down and watched people going here and there until I heard the sound of one of my favorite shows. I turned and noticed a T.V. mounted on the wall above the front desk. The show was called MTV. Although it had been on T.V. for three years, I still couldn't believe there was a show that played music videos all day and all night. We didn't have it, of course, because we didn't have cable but I got to watch it every time I visited my cousins Kissy and Jen-Jen. One time during a sleepover, my Aunt Nell let us stay up as late as we wanted. We watch videos until we no longer could hold our eyelids open. Now that was fun!

I bobbed my head to the music as I watched a familiar video until I heard someone call my name. It was Tomika's brother, Kasey. He walked toward me with a basketball propped between his arm and hip. He was one of the taller eighth grade boys and thin as a toothpick. His complexion was two shades lighter than Tomika's dark skin. Probably because they had different Dads. Everything about Kasey was skinny; his nose, the slant of his eyes. Even the shape of his face was skinny. Looking at him, you'd think his family didn't feed him much. But Tomika told me he could eat a lot. One time, she said he ate a whole pizza by himself. The only thing Tomika and her brother had in common as far as looks went was that they both had dimples. They inherited them from Tomika's mom.

"Hey Stacy. What are you doing here?" asked Kasey. He sat down next to me and set his basketball in his lap.

"My Aunt works here sometimes. She brought me and my brothers tonight for class. Is Tomika here?" I asked looking around.

"Naw. She's at home. I come to the center 'cause I play in their basketball league," he said as he threw his ball in the air. "So who's your Aunt? I might have seen her around."

"Her name is Ruthy Davis. She teaches painting," I said.

"Oh I know her! She wears that big sheet around her head."

"It's not a sheet, Kasey. It's a scarf she wears to match her clothes," I explained. At that moment, Aunt Ruthy came around the corner with a smile.

"You ready to go?" she asked.

"Yes," I said.

"Who's your friend?"

"This my best friend's brother, Kasey," I said.

"Nice to meet you Kasey. Do you visit the center often?" Aunt Ruthy asked.

"Yes ma'am. I'm on the basketball team," Kasey said. I don't know if he was trying to impress my Aunt but all of a sudden, his voice got real deep. Almost like Herman's!

"Well good. Maybe one of these days we'll check out a game. I know a few of the young men on the team. Come on, Stacy. We don't want to be late," said Aunt Ruthy.

"Uh Stacy, where's your class gonna be?" Kasey asked. I was a little shocked by his question.

"I don't know. I guess it's around the corner where my Aunt went. Why?" I asked.

He seemed a little nervous.

"Just curious. See ya later," he said and jogged off toward the gym. Funny. In all the time I've known Tomika, that was the first time Kasey and I had a real conversation.

CHAPTER TEN

When I walked into the room, I noticed a group of girls sitting on the floor against a gigantic mirrored wall. I'd never seen an entire wall covered by a mirror. If I had a mirror that big in my room, I'd be in there all day!

From first glance, it looked like there were about eight or nine girls. I noticed two girls right away, because of how they were dressed. They had those legwarmers I wanted for my birthday and they were wearing florescent sweatshirts. I immediately labeled them as the popular girls of the group and decided right then to keep my distance. Somehow, popular girls always saw me as live bait. I spotted Aunt Ruthy setting her things up for class in a corner of the room. I walked over, dropped my sweater, and sat on a near-by stool.

"Why don't you go over to the girls and introduce yourself?" said Aunt Ruthy as she sifted through some cassette tapes.

"Is there anything I can help you do before class?" I asked, hoping to avoid the inner circle.

"Nope. I got it all together. Just waiting on one more girl," she said. At that moment, another girl walked into class.

"There she is! Good evening Lalah. We were waiting on you," said Aunt Ruthy.

"Am I late?" asked Lalah.

"Nope. You're right on time," said Aunt Ruthy. She clapped her hands and sang a song as she walked over to the group. This must have been something they did at the beginning of every class because all the girls immediately got up and formed a circle while clapping and singing into position. I felt like an odd ball standing in the circle not knowing the words. I didn't want to clap my hands but I made the effort so I wouldn't look like a total dork. The girls seemed very happy to sing the song. The popular girls even did an extra move to the beat. It looked like something they had practiced outside of class. Popular girls always had good rhythm.

Out of everyone, I could hear Lalah the best. She was short and very thin, but she had a strong voice. She also had braids! That, I noticed right away and boy was I relieved! I made sure I stood next to her in the circle. The song ended and everyone clapped like a standing ovation at the end of a play. Aunt Ruthy instructed everyone to sit.

"Good evening everyone!" she said with her permanent smile. All the girls echoed her greeting. "I am so pleased to see all of you and thank you for being on time. For that, I have those delicious treats you all requested from last week. I'll pass them out at the end of class," said Aunt Ruthy. Squeals of excitement filled our inner circle when Aunt Ruthy made the announcement. "Now, before we begin, we have a visitor. She's my niece and I'm happy to have her in class with me tonight. So I would like her to start off by introducing herself and then we'll go around the circle with everyone else's name," she said. I felt my stomach drop when she put me on the spot. I cleared my throat and pretended like saying my name was no big deal.

"My name is Stacy," I said.

"Tell them your age," Aunt Ruthy said with a nudge to my arm. I thought she said I just had to say my name.

"I'm thirteen and I'm in the seventh grade," I added. Everyone said hello like they were really happy to see me. It kind'a threw me off a little. I wasn't expecting a real welcome.

"I'm Lalah. I'm 13 too and I like to dance!" she said. The other girls giggled but they weren't laughing at her. They were laughing with her. The rest of the girls said their names one at a time and told something about themselves. When we were through, Aunt Ruthy took over again.

"Since Stacy is new, let's share with her the purpose of this class. Can anyone explain what we do?" asked Aunt Ruthy. One of the popular girls shot her hand in the air, waving it back and forth.. "Yes LaShawn?" said Aunt Ruthy.

"We talk about things that are going on in the world and how it affects women. We talk about things that happen in our lives, like at school or at home and how we can handle different situations. And we talk about how to take care of ourselves," LaShawn said. She seemed pleased with her answer even before Aunt Ruthy had a chance to say if she was right or wrong.

"Very good LaShawn! What else do we do?" asked Aunt Ruthy. She pointed to a white girl in the group. She wore glasses and had long red hair that hung like ropes. She had on a plaid uniform dress and when she spoke, her teeth disappeared under two rows of metal braces.

"Like, we also dance, play games, and like, do crafts," she said. She sounded just like a Valley Girl. A Valley Girl was an expression used to describe how some people, particularly girls, spoke. They used phrases such as "like" and "for sure" in almost every sentence. I heard it all started in California, and I wondered if this girl was from California.

"Thank you Bailey. So Stacy, we are now working on sharing rites of passages for girls in different cultures. The girls can talk about their own family or they can pick a different culture to talk about. Last week Lucia shared the tradition of a Quinceanera. Her family is from Mexico. It's a big ceremony to celebrate a young girl's fifteenth birthday. It signifies her becoming a woman and all her friends and family are invited. It's almost like a wedding except the guest of honor wears pink instead of white. Lucia's Quinceanera is next year, right?' asked Aunt Ruthy.

"Yes. I can't wait! I've already picked out my dress." she said. The girls giggled.

"This week, Lalah is going to share with us what the rites of passage are in her family. She is originally from Sierra Leone," explained Aunt Ruthy. Everyone sat up extra straight, as if they were ready for a journey. I too was curious to know more about this new person. She took from her bag a manila folder, pulled out a picture and held it up for everyone to see.

"This is a picture of Sierra Leone. I have been there twice. When people think of Africa they think it looks like one big jungle but Sierra Leone has lots of mountains. My people come from the Mende tribe," she said as she held up another picture. It showed a group of women, young and old, dressed in African clothes with big jewelry. Their hair was braided in different styles and the women stood in a row like statues. "These are women of the Mende tribe. As you can see, they wear many different hairstyles. Hair is very important to the women of the Mende tribe. We take it very seriously. Braiding someone's hair is an important symbol of family bonding among the women, and it is a big part of the Sande Society rites of passage celebration," she explained.

Wow, I thought. She sounded like a teacher. As she talked, the girls quietly passed the pictures around the circle. No one talked out of turn or made fun of what she said. Everyone listened with close attention and raised their hands if they had questions. Even the popular girls!

"My Grandmother used to tell me, a woman's hair was like our crops of food. It can grow and increase only if well-tended. If it is thick, it is considered very beautiful," she said.

"How is the ceremony performed?" asked Aunt Ruthy.

"Well first, the older women begin with the scooping of rice from big barrels into bowls. They sing as they scoop the rice," she said.

"Like, what is the rice for?" asked Bailey.

"The rice is for the initiates. They will eat it at the ceremony. Each girl has what's called a sponsor. This is usually a mother, grandmother, aunt or a close friend of the family. The sponsors beat the rice in front of everyone while the initiates watch. They are not to help. Then the initiates enter the bush school at night and the town is closed to the men until the next day. Come morning, the whole community will be in town for the 'combing of the hair'.

The girls prepare by putting oil all over their body. The oil is a symbol of water. As initiates, we are thought of as being under the water like when we were carried in our mother's belly. When we come back to the village, we have come up from the water as new women. It is a new beginning. A chance to start over."

Lalah spoke with a lot of confidence for someone so young. I wanted to know more. She had a pride within that I had never seen in a person her age. Not even in Tomika. I mean, Tomika was tough, but this girl didn't have to scare anyone or be able to run fast for others to notice. You could just feel her honesty. I liked that feeling. Maybe if I owned that feeling, then I would be okay with being me.

"The ceremony begins when the sponsors braid the initiates' hair in very fancy styles. As the sponsors braid, they talk to us about growing up and being a young woman. This last picture is of my sister when she went through the ceremony last year," said Lalah. When the picture came around to me, I was shocked to see the sister's hairstyle was almost the same as mine. I actually thought she looked very pretty. Hmm, was *my* Mama a part of the Mende tribe?

"Let's give Lalah a hand for that wonderful and interesting piece of family history," said Aunt Ruthy. Everyone clapped and gave her cheers. Her story was great and after a while, I found myself not even thinking about my hair. I was just happy to be in the room and to be a part of the group.

Lalah raised her hand again.

"Yes Lalah?" said Aunt Ruthy.

"If it is alright, I would like to teach the class a dance we do at the ceremony," she said. Dancing was something I did in the privacy of my room. I was comfortable with my new company of friends, but not *that* comfortable. But I had a feeling my Aunt was going to like this idea.

CHAPTER ELEVEN

"I would be delighted to see your dance! How about it class?" asked Aunt Ruthy. I knew it. And of course, the whole class agreed. Well, maybe if I stood in the back of the class, no one would notice my one and three beat instead of a two and four. When it came to rhythm, my body always seemed to be on the odd numbers instead of the even ones. Everyone stood up and prepared themselves like a dance class warming up before rehearsal.

"Why don't we spread out and face the mirror so everyone can see themselves. Lalah, you come up front and instruct the class," said Aunt Ruthy. All the girls moved to different places in the room. I tried to remain as close to the back as possible. That is, until Aunt Ruthy noticed me and motioned for me to move a little closer. I took a few steps up and when she wasn't looking, I took one step back just to be on the safe side.

"Okay, first I will teach you the rhythm. I will clap, then you follow," said Lalah. She began to clap her hands, doing only a section at a time until we all perfected the beat. *That wasn't so bad,* I thought. I'm a good clapper. It's only when you want me to clap and move my feet at the same time that I get tangled in my steps.

"Very good. Now I will do the steps to the beat one piece at a time," instructed Lalah. She started the movements slowly, counting with each step. Everyone seemed to be catching on pretty good. I had it down until she got to the part where she added a kick-hop-turn move. I was relieved to see Bailey, the girl with the red hair, struggling on this move too. Some of the girls were confused on the timing so Lalah repeated the steps a couple of times. As I worked on the moves in the back, I could see one of the popular girls looking at me. *Oh no,* I thought, *here come the teasing and sneaky giggles.* I knew someone was bound to laugh. I just hoped they wouldn't make a big scene. Lalah walked over to the girls one at a time and helped them with the steps. I continued working until the popular girl walked over and stood in front of me.

"You having problems, too?" she asked.

"Yes," I said.

"I can help you if you like," she said. I stared at her for a minute. I couldn't believe she was offering to help.

"That would be good," I said, snapping out of my trance.

She moved beside me and took me slowly through the steps. Each time we did it, I actually got better. Her instructions were easy to follow. Not to say Lalah wasn't doing a good job. It was just nice to have a one-on-one coach. We went through the steps a few more times before Lalah stood back in front of the class to finish the dance. The popular girl said she would stay in the back with me in case I needed more help. What a relief. We did the entire dance as a class, then broke into two groups to perform in front of each other. Even though I did better than I expected, I didn't want to dance in front of the class. Lucky for me, the popular girl was in my group. We pulled second so we sat against the mirror waiting for the other group to begin. The popular girl called my name and motioned for me to sit next to her. I walked over to the empty spot and sat down.

"How do you like the class so far?" she asked.

"I like it a lot. You guys seem to have a lot of fun," I answered, feeling more at ease.

"We do! That's why I like coming here. I wish Ms. Ruthy was my aunt," said the girl. Hearing her say this about Aunt Ruthy made me feel special.

"What's your name again?" I asked, hoping not to sound too dorky.

"It's Rebecca, but people call me Becky," she said. I couldn't believe how nice she was being. She wasn't at all like I expected. I guess I made a bad judgment about her like some people often did about me. *Rule #15: Never pre-judge a person before getting to know them.*

Aunt Ruthy was right. I was glad I came. It did make me feel better about the day.

I watched group one dance the routine almost perfect. It was our turn next. I was nervous but not as much as before. In this room, I felt nobody was going to laugh or tease if I made a mistake. Lalah began to clap the beat and we started our routine. One and two and three and four. I counted over and over in my head. Before I knew it, we had finished the dance and I hadn't missed a step. Everyone clapped. I felt the need to take a bow but I held in the urge.

"Well class, we're almost out of time. There's just one more thing I wanted to do before I pass out our treats. Since Lalah has taught us this wonderful dance and the African drum class met tonight, I thought it would be if we taught them the song and perform the dance again. What do you say?" asked Aunt Ruthy. Wow, she was really testing me tonight! First, dancing in front of the class, now dancing in front of the African drum class? What next? A solo performance?

Everyone agreed with squeals and high-fives. "Don't worry, Stacy. It'll be fun. You did better than you think," said Rebecca. I guess she could tell by the look on my face that I was scared. Becky and I began gathering our jackets when Lalah joined us.

"Hey Stacy, did you have a good time?" she asked.

"Yes," I said, grabbing my coat.

"She's a little scared of dancing in front of the drum class," said Rebecca.

"Don't worry. You did good. I'll stand next to you if you want," said Lalah.

"Me too," said Rebecca.

I smiled, happy to have them in my corner. Aunt Ruthy passed out the sweet home-made chocolate chip granola bars she promised, and afterwards, we headed toward the music room. The three of us talked about different schools we attended and questioned Lalah some more about her family ceremony. The sounds of the drums grew louder as we approached the music room. When we entered, Aunt Ruthy assigned us to the front row. We stuffed our faces with chocolate and granola as we waited for the drum class to finish their session. My brothers were beating the drums as hard as they could and were doing a good job keeping up with the older boys. I couldn't believe how focused Derrick and Dean were on the instructor. I was proud to point them out to my new friends. Something I rarely did.

When the music stopped, the drum instructor turned toward us with a big smile. He was a short black man with a small round tummy, dressed in an African print shirt. He wore wiry silver metal glasses and had a small short patch of hair on his chin just like my Uncle Toris wore in his pictures from the seventies.

"We have company fellas. Ms. Ruthy, are these your lovely girls?" he said as if he was making a big announcement.

"Yes, Mr. Obadele. We have intruded on your class because I want to show you something we learned today," said Aunt Ruthy.

"Oh please, by all means. I love surprises," he said with the same smile.

"This week we talked about rites of passages for girls in different cultures and tonight Lalah shared with us a dance the women do in her family during a ceremony," explained Aunt Ruthy. "We would like to teach your drummers the beat and then have the girls perform the dance before we are dismissed for the evening."

"We would be delighted!" raved Mr. Obadele.

Aunt Ruthy called Lalah forward to teach the beat. She stood in front of the men and boys and taught them like she had been doing it for years. I just couldn't get over how unafraid she was to do anything. The drummers listened and repeated her instructions with ease. Soon, Aunt Ruthy was gathering us girls in the middle of the room to perform. I decided not to nerve up this time, but instead, pretended to have the strength of Lalah. I found a spot next to Rebecca and prepared myself to let go and have fun. Lalah walked over to us and stood beside me. I thought she would be leading the group but instead she kept her word.

"You guys ready?" asked Lalah.

"You know it," said Rebecca.

"You got the moves down Stacy?" asked Lalah.

"I think so," I said. A loud single thump signaled the drummers to start the intro. We stood at attention, ready for our opening. At the appointed time, we began to move to the rhythm. I danced with ease, feeling the beat pump through my body as if it was hitting my funny bone a thousand times. I didn't think about counting steps or wondering eyes and for the first time, it felt good. I felt joy with each step. The drummers banged faster and faster and our feet stomped the floor harder and harder until we ended in uncontrollable laughter. When the music stopped, people who had crowded around the door began to clap. I was so caught up in the dance, I didn't notice the number of people watching. At first, I wanted to hide behind Lalah but the more they clapped, the prouder I became of my performance. So when Aunt Ruthy told us to take a bow, I gladly obeyed.

Everything was fine until I looked up from my bow and saw Kasey pointing at me while talking to another boy. I forgot he was here. I was sure I'd be the butt of his jokes now. Maybe I could sneak pass without him noticing. Kasey could be silly at times, and I didn't want him saying something corny to burst my bubble. The night had been great, and I wasn't gonna let anyone ruin it.

Chapter Twelve

"Thank you ladies for a fun evening and I hope to see you all next week!" said Aunt Ruthy. Both classes began to gather their things and say goodbye to each other. Lalah, Rebecca and I walked over to our chairs to retrieve our coats.

"You coming back next week, Stacy?" asked Lalah.

"Yeah, if my mom lets me. This was fun," I said.

"Good. When you come back, I'll show you my brag book," said Rebecca.

"What's a brag book?" I asked.

"It's when you make an album filled with pictures of your friends from school and the things you did during the year," said Rebecca.

"She just wants to show you a picture of a boy she likes," Lalah teased. Rebecca's face turned red as she giggled.

"Well, we better go. My mom may be outside waiting on us," said Lalah. They began headed toward the door, until Lalah stopped and jogged back to me.

"I forgot to tell you earlier that I like your hair. Who did it for you?" she asked as Rebecca waited at the door.

"My mom," I said.

"She did a good job. It's very pretty. If you were back home, you would be the talk of the village. See ya," she said and ran back to Rebecca. Soon, they both disappeared out the door. *Wow.* I was glad to know somewhere in this world, my braids were considered cool. Aunt Ruthy put her hand on my shoulder.

"You ready to go?" she asked. I nodded.

"Okay then, take your brothers to the front and wait for me. I've got to log out before I leave," said Aunt Ruthy. I rounded my brothers up and left the room. We returned to the front desk at the entrance of the building. I instructed my brothers to sit on the bench while I stood at the desk watching music videos on the T.V.

"Say girl," said a familiar voice. I looked around and saw Kasey grinning.

"How come you still here?" I asked, looking at the T.V. I was trying to put up my guard just in case he was ready to start teasing.

"I can't hang out at the center?" he asked, spinning his basketball on his finger.

"I guess."

"You getting ready to go?"

"Yup. Just waiting on my Aunt to sign out," I said. There was an awkward silence and for a minute, I wondered why he was still standing there.

"I saw you dancing in the room," he said filling the gap. I only responded with a crooked smile. "You guys were good. I didn't know you could dance," said Kasey.

"I just learned it tonight. I was nervous though 'cause I didn't know people were going to be watching," I said.

"Well you played it off. I checked ya. It was smooth like my man M.J. That's Michael Jackson if you didn't know," he said as he nudged my arm.

"I know who M.J. is. You don't have to spell it out," I said, defending my understanding of "street talk" as Granny puts it. The awkward silence came again.

"So I heard you like Herman Price."

My eyes and mouth opened to capacity. This definitely broke our silence!

"Who told you that? Did he tell you that?" I said in desperation.

"I can't reveal my sources woman!"

"Stop playin' Kasey. Who told you that? Did Tomika say anything?" I asked.

"Okay if I say who, you can't get mad. I wasn't supposed to say anything."

"But you did, so out with the name," I demanded. Right when Kasey was about to spill the beans, my brothers started yelling as they pushed each other in a shoving match. I know I should have run over there to break it up but the anticipation of hearing what Kasey had to say was greater than being a referee. They would have to work it out on their own.

"So...," I continued.

"You promise you won't get mad?"

"Kasey! Just tell me," I said.

"Okay. Tomika told me you wanted to meet him. *But*, she only talked to me about it cause she thinks you guys aren't speaking anymore. She says you blame her for messing up the meeting between you and Herman. Guess she just wanted to talk to someone about it. And if she told *me* her problem, she *must* be sad. She don't talk to me 'bout nothing." When he finished telling me what Tomika said, he seemed eager to hear my side of the story. I didn't say anything right away. I was thinking about Tomika's feelings. Did my blow-up about the meeting Herman *really* bother her? Here I was worried about Tomika not talking to me and she was at home thinking the same thing.

"Well, are you?" Kasey asked, interrupting my thoughts.

"Am I what?"

"Are you not speaking to my sister?" he asked with a concerned look.

"No. I'm still her friend if she wants to be mine. But I am surprised she told you. It's not like I wanted anyone else to know. I wish I had never tried to meet him," I said watching my brothers closely. They had stopped fighting but I could tell by the looks on their faces and their clinched fists, the arguing wasn't over.

"Why did you then? You know, try to meet him," he asked.

"I don't know. The whole thing was a stupid idea. You're not going to spread this around, are you? I know how you like to play."

"Hey I'm not gonna say anything. You can trust me," he said.

"Then why did you bring it up?"

"Because."

"Because what?"

"Because I told Tomika the next time I saw you, I would check to see if ya'll were still cool," he said innocently. I looked at him, suspicious of his story. There was something about it that didn't sound right but I dropped the questions when I saw Aunt Ruthy turn the corner.

"There's my Aunt. I gotta go," I said.

"Sorry it took me so long," she said letting out a sigh. "I got caught up talking to Mr. Obadele about next week. We're going to combine our classes again in the second hour since we had such a good time tonight. You guys ready?" she asked, still excited from the dance. Aunt Ruthy combined her words as if they were one long sentence. Kasey and I looked at her, unsure if we were supposed to answer.

"I got front seat," said Derrick.

"No you don't! Get in the back," I said as we headed toward the front door.

"See ya, Stacy," Kasey yelled. I turned around to see him still trying to spin the ball on his finger. I wanted to tell him again not to say anything to his friends but decided not to bother. The damage was probably already done.

"Bye Kasey. Tell Tomika I'll see her tomorrow."

I tagged Dean as I went through the door and took off, leaving him desperately trying to catch up. We ran around the car until Aunt Ruthy unlocked the door.

"Let's get in kids. I've got to get you guys back home before dinner," said Aunt Ruthy. We jumped in the car and in no time, we were on our way home.

"Can I come back next week, Aunt Ruthy?" I asked.

"So you did have a good time?" I nodded with a smile.

"That young man at the counter, was he the same boy from earlier?" asked Aunt Ruthy.

"Yes."

"Well he sure did enjoy the dance. He was grinning from ear-to-ear. I started to ask him to get out there and join us," Aunt Ruthy said. I laughed hard at the thought of Kasey trying to dance.

"Aunt Ruthy you're funny," I said.

"Did the center help you forget about today?" asked Aunt Ruthy.

"It did. I like your class. Everybody was nice to me," I said.

"Why wouldn't they be? You're a nice young lady yourself. Don't you think so?" asked Aunt Ruthy.

"Yeah but I always feel like the weirdo of the group. But tonight, everyone was cool. Even the ones I thought were going to give me a hard time turned out to be really nice. That girl Lalah, she was the nicest of them all. She even said she liked my hair," I said.

"You see. You're not the only girl in the world who gets their hair braided. You are a beautiful young woman Stacy. Those girls didn't speak to you because of the way you look. They spoke to you tonight because they don't feel the need to insult someone to make themselves feel good. Besides, they know I don't allow no mess," Aunt Ruthy said with sass.

We sang songs and told corny knock-knock jokes all the way home. Aunt Ruthy talked to Dad for a little while before leaving. At dinner, my brothers and I stepped on each other's sentences, trying to be the first to tell Dad the events of the evening. Pleased with how much we enjoyed ourselves, he said could go back next week. Mom hadn't made it home from work before it was time for bed. I would just have to tell her about the center tomorrow. I was pooped anyway and was looking forward to a good night's rest. Instead of the usual dream about Herman, I re-lived in my mind the dance steps to the beat of the drums. With each move, I slipped deeper into sleep.

Chapter Thirteen

I awoke to a loud buzz and shot up like Pop-Rock candy. Looking around, I realized it was just the alarm clock going off. Was it time for school already? I reached over and hit the off button then plopped back down in bed. Five more minutes of sleep was all I wanted but the sudden urge to use the bathroom took hold of me.

After I finished my morning business, I stood at the sink washing my hands and caught a glimpse of myself in the mirror. I began examining my braids. The more I stared, the more I couldn't stop staring. I mean, I never really looked at them before now. Guess I was trying to avoid seeing what I thought was ugly.

I turned my head sideways and watched the braids and beads dangle towards the floor. I turned them in every direction: profile, up, down, backwards. I grabbed a mirror from the drawer and looked at the patterns at the top of my head. I got so caught up with my hair, I began acting like a supermodel, posing in the mirror as if people were taking pictures of me. The thought of myself as "cute" dared to enter my mind. I spoke into the brush as if it were a microphone, answering questions to imaginary fans until I was startled by Dean standing in the doorway yarning.

"What are you doing?" he asked in a sleepy voice.

"Don't worry about what I'm doing. What do you want?" I said, trying to yell in a low voice.

"I gotta use the bathroom," he whined as he started toward the toilet.

"Go use the one downstairs," I said, stopping him with my microphone.

"It's dark down there! I'm scared!" Dean yelled.

"Shhh. Be quiet before you wake up everybody," I said rushing Dean to the toilet.

"What are you two doing?" Mom said, standing in the doorway. I forgot she was usually the one who woke up first. When I saw Mama, I felt really happy to see her again. It seemed like she had been gone for a long time.

"Good morning, Mama!" I said cheerfully.

"Good morning," she said with a suspicious eye. "Why are you up so early? I usually have to drag you out of bed," she said focusing on Dean's pajamas, which were on backwards.

"I don't know. Just woke up early today," I said.

"Well since you're up, you might as well start getting ready." She gently guided Dean, who was still sleepy, to his room.

I brushed my teeth, admired my hair one more time in the mirror and went back to my room. When I walked in, there it was on the bed. The cutest pink jogging suit I had ever seen! I ran to the bed in disbelief and picked up the outfit. Yes! It was in my size. I sprinted into Mama's room where she stood at the bathroom counter combing her hair.

"Is this outfit for me, Mama?"

"It's not for your brother. I don't think he looks good in pink," she said putting on mascara. "You said you had to re-take pictures so I got something nice for you to wear." *Uh-oh.* Why did she have to say that? I forgot about my lie and now I felt bad for making her believe that story. I don't know why, but I felt I needed to tell the truth. *Rule #5: Tell the truth, no matter the consequences.* Something in me just wouldn't sit right with the lie.

"Mama, I don't have to take pictures again," I said with my head hung low.

"What do you mean?"

"I wanted you to straighten my hair but you said no so I had to come up with a reason for you to do it. Tomika was gonna tell this boy that I liked him and I wanted..." Mama interrupted and finish the sentence.

"You wanted to impress him. All this over a boy?"

"Yes ma'am. I mean, I didn't want him to be my boyfriend cause I know that's against the rules. I just wanted him to think I was cute. I'm sorry," I said nearly in tears.

"You know you are not allowed to have a boyfriend!" she said with fury. I could tell she was getting ready to let me have it but right when I thought she was about to explode, she stopped talking. There was silence for a moment and then she spoke.

"Stacy, you're cute with straight hair or hair that's braided. Either way, it's not the hair that makes you beautiful, it's your personality. But if you don't like who you are, neither will anyone else you're trying to impress. Boys come and go but there is only one Stacy Michelle Bell. So you better get to liking her and stop worrying about what some pea-headed little boy thinks of you. I like you. As a matter of fact, I love you," Mama said as she managed to raise a little smile at me.

Her words made me feel a little stronger. Safer. The kind of feeling you get when you think you're in a lot of trouble and then everything turns out okay. Don't get me wrong, I still wanted to impress Herman, but I wasn't worried about it so much anymore. I also saw Mama in a different way. She reminded me of the women Lalah talked about in her family. The wise elderly women who were willing to listen to the young girls being initiated. Maybe she wasn't so clueless after all.

"Thanks for the outfit Mama. Can I wear it today?" I nervously asked.

"Yes Stacy, you may wear it today. Now go on and get ready for school. I've got to go before I'm late," Mama said. She buttoned her blouse, grabbed her jacket and purse and tapped Dad on his foot. "Get up James and get the boys ready," she said heading for the door.

"Mama?" She stopped at the door. "Will you teach me how to braid, maybe this week-end?" I asked. She smiled with surprise.

"*You* want to learn how to braid?" I nodded. "Okay, we will give it a go on Saturday."

Chapter Fourteen

I couldn't help standing in the mirror star-gazing at myself once again. My pink jogging suit fit me perfectly and blended well with the beads in my hair. I added my favorite pair of earrings to complete the look. With the way I felt, I was looking forward to the school. I grabbed my book bag and went downstairs for breakfast. No need for a hat today!

When I got to the kitchen, Dad and the boys were stuffing their faces with cereal and coffee. Coffee, yuk! I didn't understand how adults could drink that stuff. It tasted like a strong cup of mud with sugar sprinkled on top.

I was too excited to join Dad and my brothers for a sit down breakfast. Instead, I heated a pop tart and wrapped it in a napkin on my way to the car. Dad locked up the house as my brothers and I piled into the car. The boys began their usual morning fuss in the back seat. Dad settled in the driver's seat and started the engine, letting it rumble a bit while he turned on the radio and adjusted it to his favorite radio station. As we backed out the driveway, I felt the subtle heat from the morning sun bounce off the window, warming my face and scalp. Today was going to be 69 degrees and sunny.

"What are you smiling about over there?" asked Dad.

"Nothing. Just happy it's warm today," I said looking out the window.

"You got that right. Are you okay?" he asked.

"Yeah," I said with a chuckle. "Why you ask?"

"Well, yesterday didn't seem like a very good day for you. Just wanted to know if everything was better now?"

"I'm okay," I said. It made me feel good to see that he cared. Dads. They may not always understand, but they care.

"Oh, that's my song! You remember that song Stacy? You used to like me to sing it to you when we lived over by your grandmother," Daddy said as he popped his fingers. Dad's oldies radio station may not have been my favorite, but I did remember that song. It brought back memories so I sung along with him. By the time we pulled up to the school, we were all in harmony like a singing group. When the last note was sung, I gathered my things and said good-bye.

"Have a good day, honey. By the way, you look nice," he said with a big grin. "Thanks Daddy," I said and closed the door.

I took a deep breath of the cool crisp morning air as I looked around the school yard, then walked over to my usual spot. Leaning against the wall, I unwrapped the pop tart from the napkin and continued my breakfast. Soon after, I saw the buses coming around the corner. But I wasn't concerned. I just ate the pop tart, waiting. A couple of kids filed off the bus first, then Tomika appeared. As usual, she was well dressed. When she noticed me, I could she was impressed as she walked over.

"Hey. I like your outfit," she said sounding surprised to see me in the latest fashion.

"Thanks. My Mama gave it to me this morning. Want some?" I asked breaking off a piece of pop tart.

"I see you couldn't get your mom to take the braids out," said Tomika as took a small bite of the pop tart.

"I didn't ask. I don't mind them anymore," I said, watching the school yard fill with students.

"You don't? Yesterday you acted liked you were embarrassed!"

"I was at first, but I like them now," I said, tossing the last piece of tart in my mouth. Tomika didn't say anything. She just stared at me as if she didn't know my name.

"What? Why are you looking at me like that?" I asked. I thought maybe I had crumbs around my mouth so I wiped it with the back of my hand.

"No reason. I mean, if you're okay with the braids then I'm okay with it," said Tomika. Even though I wasn't sure if that was true, I knew she was trying to be nice. Deep down inside, we both wanted to apologize. But small talk and moments of silence was our way of saying *sorry*.

I decided since everything was cool between us, and my confidence was up, I would dare to do the unspeakable. I would enter the school using the side door. That meant I had to walk past The Wall. The idea alone made my heart beat a little faster but I felt I was up for the test. So without much thought, I asked, "You want to wait by the side doors?"

"*You* want to walk over to the side doors? Why?" Tomika said with suspicion.

"We always get shoved when the bell rings going in the front doors. I'm tired of being pushed back and forth. It would be easier just to go through the side doors. Nobody hardly ever goes that way," I said hoping that was her last question. Unfortunately, it wasn't. She twisted her mouth in her usual way when she felt I wasn't telling the truth.

"Come on. What's really going on? You want to walk in front of *Herman*?"

"If you think so. I just want to go through the side doors," I said, sticking to my story.

"Okay then, let's go," Tomika dared. We picked up our book bags and headed across the yard. Tomika walked a step behind as if she was anticipating me calling it off. But I kept walking, keeping my eyes on an old leafless oak tree by the basketball courts, hoping no one would notice us. We were almost past Herman and his crew when I heard his voice calling Tomika's name. *Oh no.* I wanted to keep walking and wait for Tomika by the doors but once again, I couldn't move. We both watched him jog over to us. *Play it cool*, I told myself.

"Hey Tomika," he said.

"What's up Herman?" said Tomika. I knew he wasn't there to talk to me, but this time I wasn't bothered as much.

"Hey Stacy," he said as he looked me straight in the eyes. I quickly turned my head toward him, trying not to look surprised.

"Hi." That's all I could get out, but it was enough.

"Did you guys finish your paper for Mrs. Carter's class?" Herman asked. He spoke as if the three of us always talked before school. I couldn't believe how casual he was acting. Tomika said yes while I simply nodded.

"Have you finished?" Tomika asked.

"Naw. I'll write the ending at lunch. No biggie," he said, looking around the yard. For a split second, there was silence. Then with all my energy, I took control of the moment.

"Well, we gotta go. The bell is about to ring," I said. I grabbed Tomika's arm and pulled her toward our mission, leaving Herman Price standing alone.

"Bye Herman!" Tomika said, laughing as we hurried to the door. When we got around the corner, I let out a huge sigh! We both began to laugh.

"Girrrll! I can't believe you did that!" Tomika said, bending over from laughing hard.

"I can't believe I did that either! I mean, nobody was saying anything and I didn't want to keep standing there so I ended it. Did you see the way he looked?" I asked. The laughter kept coming until tears rolled down our faces.

"Yeah. He was surprised we left him by himself," Tomika squeaked out in the middle of laughter.

"Why did he come over asking that question?"

"Maybe he knows something about the note and was trying to see if we knew who wrote it," said Tomika.

"You think it's him?"

Tomika shrugged her shoulders. The bell rang. We gathered our things and opened the doors with ease. No pushing. No shoving.

Chapter Fifteen

The school day had been a breeze. I went to class as usual, talked to friends, hung out with Tomika and even got a few compliments about my hair. Wow! What a difference a little attitude can make.

At lunch, I took out my paper for Mrs. Carter's class to check for misspelled words and incorrect grammar. Mrs. Carter couldn't stand bad grammar. As I read through it, the report sounded sad. The topic of the paper was "What Does Beauty Mean?" But my paper should have said "What Does Ugly Mean?" because there was *nothing* beautiful about it. I guess writing it after Mama announced she was braiding my hair wasn't the best time to talk about beauty.

After reading it, I wanted to change the words to express a different feeling. I decided to re-write the paper before class. Lucky for me, I had gym fifth period. I asked Coach Taylor if I could finish my paper during class instead of participating in free-play. Being known as the "good student" had its privileges because he gave me a pass to the library without questions. I knew I didn't have much time so I wrote quickly but was careful to choose the right words. To my surprise, everything I wanted to say poured out with ease. I don't think I ever looked up until the bell rung for sixth period. Before leaving, I proof-read the paper and smiled, satisfied with my work.

When I got to the room, most of the students had already arrived. Some were goofing off as usual but most were looking over their reports. Tomika was seated at the desk looking through her folder.

"Hey. You got here fast," I said. Tomika didn't respond. She just kept flipping paper after paper. "What's wrong?" I asked.

"I can't find my report," she said.

"Well, maybe because you're looking in your History folder. This is English," I said. Tomika stopped and looked on the outside of the folder. It read: *History*. She gave a big sigh and began to laugh while pulling out her English folder. When she opened it, sure enough, there was her paper.

"Girl, I'm just nervous. I hate reading in front of the class. I don't know why we can't just turn it in," Tomika said. She looked frustrated. I, on the other hand, was calm.

The bell rang and everyone got situated in their seats. Mrs. Carter, who had been guarding the hallway, stepped in and closed the door behind her. She set her coffee mug on the corner of her desk and walked to the lectern that was placed in the front of the room.

"Good afternoon class. I do hope you all have your assignments prepared and ready to read aloud. I also hope you followed my directions. The last few periods were a bit disappointing. Directions were not followed and a few students talked about everything except their personal opinions of beauty. So, for your sakes, I hope you are better prepared. With that said, I shall call the first presenter," she said adjusting her glasses.

Everyone sat straight up in their seats, praying they wouldn't be the first to speak. I was comfortable, but I didn't want to go first. "Miss Stacy Bell, please come to the lectern," she said. I felt a lump drop from my throat to my stomach. Slowly, I slid out of the seat, gathered my papers and walked to the front of the room. I glanced to the side where Mrs. Carter was sitting in a chair waiting to be impressed. Then I made eye contact with Tomika who looked more afraid than me. I took a deep breath and began reading.

When I would hear the word beauty, I used to think of a famous model or my grandmother's flower garden. I thought of a lot of different things, but I never thought of me. I thought the word meant how something looked. Not what it felt like. I thought it meant the latest hairstyles, make-up and cute clothes. I thought if I had all of these things, I would feel beautiful and people would see me as beautiful.

But I've learned from family, and a few new friends, the true meaning of beauty. Now I think it can mean knowing who you are and liking yourself. When my favorite Aunt and I are together, she calls me her Queen. This makes me feel beautiful. Singing old songs with my Dad in the car makes me feel good. And even though we are not the best singers, the time we share is beautiful. When my Mama braids my hair, she believes it makes me beautiful. At first, I didn't like braids because it wasn't what everyone else was wearing. But after meeting a girl named Lalah at the community center, I found out braids are a part of an African tradition. Her family is originally from Sierra Leone. She explained how important the tradition of braiding was in her culture. Hearing her speak about this made me feel special since we both had braids. It felt like I was connected to people far away from America. Now I like my braids not because they are different, but because I feel good when I wear them.

Beauty is who you are, not what you are. It is not just what you can see but what you can feel. Beauty, to me, is love from family and friends.

With all the confidence I could find, I challenged myself to look at my peers. Everyone was quiet, even Mrs. Carter. I picked up the report and walked back to my seat feeling like I had just accomplished something in my seventh grade life. Of course, this didn't mean I was about to be the topic of hallway gossip. It simply meant, for the first time, I was proud myself.

After a short delay, Mrs. Carter rose to her feet, clapping her hands with excitement. All heads turned in sync, staring at the unusual display of happiness on Mrs. Carter's face.

"Very original Miss Bell! Very original indeed! Thank you for your honesty. Alright, who's next?" she said looking at her grade book once more. I glanced over at Tomika who also approved my speech with a smile. I could tell she was proud to have me as her friend.

Everyone finished their reports before dismissal. When the bell rang, I jumped up ready to leave. Tomika pushed through the herd of students rushing to free themselves from the confinement of school and made it over to my desk.

"Girl! You did a good job on your paper. She's gonna give you an A. I couldn't have said all of that! I'll be lucky to get a C after what you read," said Tomika.

"Don't sweat it. You did good too," I said, checking my area to make sure I had everything. I began stuffing my binder in my backpack when I saw Herman walking toward my desk.

"What's up, Tomika?" Herman said, leaning on his favorite leg for support. Butterflies I thought I had locked away, suddenly broke free at the sound of his voice and scattered throughout my body. Instead of looking into those hazel-green eyes, I just kept messing with my backpack, pretending to be busy.

"Hey Herman," Tomika said with a tease in her voice.

"Have you seen your brother?" he asked.

"He's around here somewhere. Why? You got something to tell him?" Tomika said.

"Yeah, but I'll catch up with him at the apartments," Herman said. I was praying he would leave after his last question because I was running out of things to do. Then it happened again. He spoke to me!

"Uh, hey Stacy." My heart was beating fast as I forced my eyes in his direction. "I liked your report," Herman said with half a smile. *Wow!* Herman Price was smiling at me!

"Thanks," I said flashing my own smile. But not too big. Didn't want to overdo it and look desperate.

"Tomika can I talk to you outside?" he asked. He peeked at me again as if he knew something I didn't know.

"Sure," Tomika said, glancing back at me. She grabbed her things and walked into the hallway with him. *Now what is that all about*, I wondered? Is this the moment he finally confesses to be the mystery writer? Maybe since he knows I know how he feels, he's too shy to say it face to face. He's probably telling Tomika everything he wants her to tell me. What if he gives her his number to give to me? I can't call him. I'm not allowed to talk to boys on the phone. Another one of Mama's '*you're not old enough*' rules. Should I stand here and wait for Tomika to come back or walk pass them as if I don't know anything?

Mrs. Carter called my name, breaking the series of rambling questions in my head.

"Stacy, can I see you for a moment?" she said with a stern look on her face. What had I done to deserve that look? I thought she said my paper was good. I dragged my feet toward her desk and stood with my back to the door. I wanted to make sure our meeting would be private.

"If you don't mind me asking, what made you write those things in your paper?"

"Well…," I said, unsure if this was a trick question. "I really did think beauty was like the women I saw in magazines or on T.V. But after sitting in a class for girls at the community center last night, I started to think about how I felt. You know, like when you're happy and people make you feel good then you think you look good. So I thought about all the things I like doing and all the people I like to be with and thought, that could be beautiful too. I figure beauty don't have to be, I mean, *doesn't* have to be what you look like. Beauty can be how a person feels." I couldn't tell if I had given the answer she was looking for because she was quiet as if she was chewing on my words to see if they were properly seasoned. And then she did what we students rarely got a chance to see. She smiled so big, I could see most of her teeth!

"Well now, aren't you the scholar! Great job Miss Bell. Not too many kids your age, as well as adults, realize the true meaning of beauty. You keep that attitude young lady and it will take you a long way." She patted me on the arm and turned back to her desk, marking papers with her signature red ink.

I blew a sigh of relief as I turned to leave. Eager to get back to Tomika, I hoped they were through speaking by the time I stepped into the hallway. Lucky for me, Tomika was standing alone. Now the mystery would finally be solved. But as I approached Tomika, she didn't look like she had good news. In fact, the closer I got, the more nervous she became.

"What's wrong?" I asked.

"Nothing."

"Are you sure?" She didn't answer right away. Instead, she looked down at the floor, rubbing her Penny Loafers together.

"Well? What did he say? Did he write the note?" I asked, becoming impatient.

"No," she said, still looking down at her feet.

"Are you sure? Did he tell you that?"

"Uh-huh," she said. Before I could ask the next question, a bus rider jogged pass, announcing the buses were running late. The news gave me more time to pry the truth from Tomika. It was pretty obvious she was holding something back.

"I have to be standing in my group when the bus comes," she said looking off. I thought it was weird for her to turn away while talking to me. This was never a problem before. But I was not letting her out of this so easily.

"I'll walk with you to your group," I said. She didn't say no and she didn't say okay. She just picked up her bag and we headed down hall.

"So if he didn't write the note, then what did he want to talk to you about?"

"I don't know how to say it."

"Just say it," I said. We pushed open the double doors and stepped outside. There were kids hanging around everywhere on the east lawn. Most were waiting on the buses, except for the Walkers. They always lingered a little longer in the school yard, when the buses were late, to run around with the Riders. The monitors were talking on walkie-talkies while chasing kids, trying to keep order. Tomika and I walked over to our spot, keeping distance from the others. I guess everyone was running late because I looked toward the front expecting to see Daddy but he wasn't there. We dropped our heavy book bags and leaned against the brick wall. Like everyone else, I too was forced to wait. Wait on Daddy...and wait on Tomika to speak.

Chapter Sixteen

"Herman asked me for my number," Tomika said looking at the kids in the yard. I couldn't believe the words that had spilled from her mouth. My stomach dropped after knowing the truth.

"So it's *you* he likes?" I didn't mean to sound so surprised but I couldn't help it. Here we were plotting how to make him like me and turns out, he liked Tomika the whole time! Boy did I feel like a goof-ball. I was scared to ask the next question but I needed to know even if it meant getting my feelings crushed more than they already were.

"Did you give it to him?"

"No. I told him I couldn't because I had a friend that liked him and it wouldn't be right," she said, finally looking me in the eyes. *Wow.* She always did take up for me. I had to admit, I was happy she turned him down but part of me was sorry I was the reason for her decision. What girl at Forest Hill Middle School wouldn't want him rubbing shoulders with her down the halls to class. I didn't feel right taking that prize away. It's not like she was trying to get him to like her, it just happened. So I decided to be the one to cover my feelings for *her* sake. For once in our friendship, I wanted to be the protector.

"It's cool Tomika. It really is. In a way, its kinda funny. Us doing all that planning and he was liking you the whole time. No wonder he kept coming over. He was trying to look at you!" I said nudging her arm. She laughed a bit, embarrassed by the truth. I rarely saw this side of Tomika. Her tough layer peeled back.

"Do you like him?" I asked.

"I don't know. I mean, I ain't never looked at him like that. He's just my brother's friend. I'm kinda glad I had an excuse not to give him my number. My Mama *says* it's okay, but she gets mad when boys call. So I don't even bother."

"What you gonna do?" I asked, curious to know her next step.

"What am *I* gonna do? What are *you* gonna do?" asked Tomika.

"Do about what?"

"The note! We still don't know who wrote it," she said, cleverly turning the question back to me. Knowing the truth about Herman's feelings distracted me from that piece of the puzzle. But by now, I was beginning not to care about knowing. It had all been too much. My hair issues, trying to be popular and keep friendships, a note from a secret admirer, confessing secret crushes and trying to cover my lie to Mama was more than I planned. After going through all of that, I was just happy to be friends with Tomika again. That's what really mattered. Sure, I was disappointed that I wasn't the love of Herman's life but I could always go back to my dream bubbles and no one would ever have to know.

"The buses are here!" a boy screamed. All the bus riders began running around until they were in four single lines. The monitors, who were angry they had to stay longer than their normal working hours, were yelling on their bullhorns, instructing the Walkers to go home and the Riders to make sure they had all their belongings.

"If you leave something behind, then just go to Lost and Found tomorrow," they yelled.

"I gotta go. See you later," Tomika said as she picked up her book bag and began walking to the third line. Before she reached the row, she turned around, walking backwards as she spoke. "Call me tonight if you find out about the note!"

I shook my head and laughed to myself as I walked around the corner to the front of the school and sat on the steps to wait for Dad. I took out a book I got from the library last week and flipped to chapter five. After reading the first sentence, I heard someone say my name. It was Kasey. He did a light jog over to me, carrying his basketball.

"Hey Stacy. Did my sister get on the bus?"

"Yeah, she just left. How come you're not on the bus?" I asked.

"Sometimes I ride, sometimes I walk home when I'm gonna play some b-ball after school," he said spinning the ball on his finger like he was trying to show off. I figured he said what he wanted to say so I went back to reading.

"You waiting on your ride?" he asked.

"Yeah," I said without looking up. He bounced the ball off the brick wall a couple of times before disturbing me again.

"Say, did a boy come up to you the other day and hand you a note?" he asked. I could tell by the quiver in his voice he was nervous. Now *that,* got my attention.

"Yeah. How did you know?" I asked.

"That was my friend Reggie," he said with a sneaky grin.

"Why would your friend give me a note like that?" I asked. I was almost afraid of the answer.

"Let's just say he was doing me a favor," he said, twisting his ball in the air. I couldn't believe it! *Kasey* wrote the note! I didn't know how to feel about the situation. It was awkward. My best friend's brother liked me?

"Surprised huh," he said. I nodded, feeling warm blood rush to my cheeks. "I always thought you were nice. Just didn't know how to say it I guess," he said looking away. "You look cute today," he added.

"Thanks," I said. The words almost didn't make it out of my mouth. Thank God at that moment I heard Dad's car horn. I gathered my things and jumped up to leave.

"Gotta go," I said, quickly walking away. Before I could get too far, he called my name again. I wanted to keep going and act like I didn't hear him, but I couldn't hurt his feelings, so I stopped and turned around.

"Can I walk you to first period on Monday?" he asked. I thought for a minute and then nodded. What could it hurt? Maybe he wasn't so goofy after all. *Wow.* My first escort to class!

I stepped it double-time to the car and got in. After I locked my the door, Dad checked for cars then pulled away from the curb. I stared at Kasey through the side mirror as we drove off. He didn't walk away until we were almost down the street.

"Hey baby girl. You have a good day?" Dad asked.

"Yeah," I said with a huge smile.

Chapter Seventeen

The sun continued to shine late into the afternoon. It was like God held it out a little longer for me so I could remember the day. Everything ending so well that when my corny brothers asked me to go bike riding with them I actually said yes. Sometimes I can tolerate being around them. I hadn't ridden my bike in a long time. You know how it is; when you get older, you put away things you think are childish.

We all hopped on our bikes and headed down the slope of the driveway into the street. As the wind blew in my face, I couldn't resist the temptation to lift my hands in the air just to see if I could still ride without holding the handle bars. Yup! I still had the skills and it felt good. We rode all over the neighborhood. Competing to see who could pump up the hills without stopping and who was brave enough to keep pumping as we rode down. We took a pit stop at the corner store to buy bubble gum, Chick-O-Sticks and Jolly Ranchers. We stayed out until the street lights popped on one by one as if Mama was operating the ON switch herself. I told my brothers it was time to head back and challenged them to a race.

Mama was already home. I couldn't wait to tell her about Mrs. Carter's comments on my report and about Herman liking Tomika. I left out the part about Kasey. I wanted to save that news for Tomika. But before I could call her, Mama wanted to hear my English report.

"Stacy, that was absolutely beautiful!" she said once I finished reading. She gave me a big hug. The kind of hug parents give when they want you to feel the pride they have for you.

"So are you ready for your first lesson in hair braiding? I thought we'd start early," Mama asked.

"Can I call Tomika first?"

"Go ahead. But don't be too long," she warned.

"I won't," I said as I ran to the kitchen. When Tomika answered I immediately jumped into, "Guess what?" After hearing who the Secret Admirer was, Tomika burst into laughter. She couldn't believe it was her brother. I begged her not to say anything because I knew she would use the news as kryptonite against her brother. But I'm sure he knew she was gonna find out sooner or later. After all, we *were* best friends.

With the case solved and all the questions answered, I hung up the phone and gathered all the tools needed for my first lesson. Using my old Barbie head, Mama carefully instructed me through the steps. Three strands of hair crossing over and under while weaving in the sectioned hair hanging below until a cornrow had formed. "Not bad for your first time," she would say as I practiced the rows.

There were many more practice sessions with Mama on the weekends and some private sessions with just me and the doll in my room. Pretty soon I began to construct my own designs in my hair, looking through magazines to get ideas. I even practiced a few times on Tomika. She liked for me to braid her hair into two corn rows when she had a basketball game.

As the weeks carried on, that embarrassing day became a forgetful blur. Kasey turned out to be really fun. He taught me basketball and I helped him with his homework sometimes when he waited with me after school. Of course, I wasn't allowed to date boys in middle school but we held hands whenever we could. Tomika decided she would let Herman be her escort in the hallways but when he touched her in a place she didn't feel comfortable during lunch, she quickly let him know, with a shove to the chest, she wasn't ready to be *that* popular.

"He's so stupid," she said to me after explaining what happened. I knew that meant she was ready to cut him loose.

"Mama," I said during one of our sessions. "I think I'm going teach the girls in my class at the community center how to braid."

"Is that right." Mama said while paying attention to my hands.

"Yes," I said.

"What made you think of doing that?"

"Cause, I think every girl should know how to braid, no matter what color you are," I said plaiting the hair at the bottom.

"Continue," she said, now focusing on me. She became curious and surprised at the same time.

"Well, braiding is hard at first and not too pretty when you don't know what you're doing. But if you keep working at it, you can make some pretty cool styles for yourself. And once you learn how to do it, you'll never forget; like riding a bike. That's something any girl can learn." When I finished the braid, Mama was grinning from ear to ear. Like I had accomplished something really important.

"Stacy, I think you finally got it."

Rule #1: Learn to like who you are...always.

THE END